ISBN 978-1-330-72196-4
PIBN 10096924

This book is a reproduction of an important historical work. Forgotten Books uses
state-of-the-art technology to digitally reconstruct the work, preserving the original format
whilst repairing imperfections present in the aged copy. In rare cases, an imperfection in
the original, such as a blemish or missing page, may be replicated in our edition. We do,
however, repair the vast majority of imperfections successfully; any imperfections that
remain are intentionally left to preserve the state of such historical works.

1 MONTH OF
FREE
READING

at
www.ForgottenBooks.com

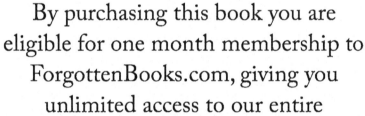

By purchasing this book you are eligible for one month membership to ForgottenBooks.com, giving you unlimited access to our entire collection of over 700,000 titles via our web site and mobile apps.

To claim your free month visit:

www.forgottenbooks.com/free96924

English
Français
Deutsche
Italiano
Español
Português

www.forgottenbooks.com

Mythology Photography **Fiction**
Fishing Christianity **Art** Cooking
Essays Buddhism Freemasonry
Medicine **Biology** Music **Ancient**
Egypt Evolution Carpentry Physics
Dance Geology **Mathematics** Fitness
Shakespeare **Folklore** Yoga Marketing
Confidence Immortality Biographies
Poetry **Psychology** Witchcraft
Electronics Chemistry History **Law**
Accounting **Philosophy** Anthropology
Alchemy Drama Quantum Mechanics
Atheism Sexual Health **Ancient History**
Entrepreneurship Languages Sport
Paleontology Needlework Islam
Metaphysics Investment Archaeology
Parenting Statistics Criminology
Motivational

THE MURDER OF EDWIN DROOD

RECOUNTED BY JOHN JASPER

BEING

An Attempted Solution of the Mystery based on
Dickens' Manuscript and Memoranda.

BY

PERCY T. CARDEN

WITH

AN INTRODUCTION.

BY

B. W. MATZ.

G. P. PUTNAM'S SONS
NEW YORK
1920

PRINTERS :

WHITEHEAD AND MILLER, LTD.,

LEEDS.

INDEX.

—

LIST OF ILLUSTRATIONS.

———

INTRODUCTION

BY

B. W. MATZ.

NEVER having attempted to solve the wonderful mystery woven into Dickens' unfinished story, and thereby being innocent of marked prejudices regarding the numerous knotty problems it presents to those who delve deeply into its intricacies, I have no misgivings in complying with the invitation to write a few prefatory words to this, the latest endeavour to unravel the tangled threads of the story's fabric.

. I am, however, an enthusiastic student of the problem, content with the fascination derived from following the many by-ways traversed by all those who seek to lead others to a solution. That there have been many such guides a long row of books and pamphlets bear witness. Alluring in themselves, each book in its own different way contributes something to the intellectual exercise which the minute study of the subject offers.

I suppose every reader of *Edwin Drood* laments bitterly that it comes to so abrupt an end, and few lay it aside without some thought as to how it was to terminate had Dickens lived to finish it. Many devote to the mystery something more than the concession of a passing thought, and some attempt with scholarly instinct to unravel its mysteries for themselves, and evolve theories concerning its probable ending until they are caught by the fever of its subtle spell. And so the readers of the book are divided into two classes : those who are badly attacked by the fever and those who prove to be immune. The former have come to be dubbed " Droodists," and it is for these that scientific efforts to solve the problem, of which Mr. Carden's is one, have their chief interest and attraction. Although the one and true solution may never definitely be discovered, there is no doubt that every fresh study of the book reveals something helpful towards that end, and for that reason has its particular value. In this way, one point, hitherto debatable, has been established with sufficient surety to put it beyond doubt : John Jasper actually murdered his nephew. Mr. Carden starts off from that hypothesis, and I am naturally in complete agreement with him on that point.

The other main question which confronts and baffles all students is that of the Datchery assumption. That Datchery is one of the characters of the book in disguise is generally agreed, and each of those who could possibly have filled that role has in turn been suggested, and the individual cases presented and argued by previous writers. The weeding out process leaves as most likely Helena Landless, Bazzard and Tartar. The strongest claim has been for Helena Landless, whilst Bazzard has been a favourite second. Mr. Carden chooses Tartar, and his case for the sailor is much the best that has yet been presented. In arriving at this conclusion he is able also to find an important part for Helena to perform quite in keeping with the peculiar and distinctive traits in her character, traits which

Dickens so often insists in revealing, and chiefly for which she has been singled out as the fitting person to enact the part. Bazzard too, is found work by Mr. Carden suitable to his disposition and far more in keeping with his nature than that of playing at being a detective.

But Mr. Carden's book appeals to me as one of the most important contributions to the subject by virtue of the fact that he has read and studied carefully every word of the manuscript and of the notes which Dickens prepared for his own guidance, and has collated them with the printed book. The result is his discovery of certain erasures and alterations in the manuscript which help him to come to certain conclusions, not possible without this close study and comparison. These include certain passages which Dickens wrote and which were not published, one of which refers to Durdles's yard, and the possibility of Jasper availing himself of it in conjunction with his use of quick-lime in the execution of his deed. He also has been able to locate at Rochester the site of Durdles's yard, which makes his theory regarding the manner of the murder and the attempted concealment of it locally quite possible.

His reading too of the cover design is most ingenious and quite consistent with his theory. The figure kneeling to Rosa on the left hand side he claims to be Neville Landless, for he discovers internal evidence that Neville had a moustache—a real piece of the Sherlock Holmes method.

But perhaps the most important and interesting discovery he has made is the exact date of the story which almost eerily fits the context in every detail, including even the topography of Rochester and the neighbourhood at the time the story was being enacted. This enables him to work out the complete chronology of events to the surmounting of the hitherto arguable point concerning the phrase " at about this time," at the beginning of chapter xviii.

Altogether, Mr. Carden has made a notable contribution to the solution of the ever green and ever baffling puzzle, and although, of course, it is not supposed that everyone will be in agreement with his theories, few will dispute the care and reason he employs in stating his case or his competency to deal with the whole problem.

Mr. Carden is a newcomer in the game as he calls it —a game the greatest danger to which he thinks is lest it should one day end in a complete solution. In the meantime, he enters the centre court, and with his effective strokes, fresh methods and new ideas, is sure to stimulate the other players and attract the onlookers, for throughout he exhibits a sane, good-natured and dignified attitude. For these reasons his performance is worthy of careful study and consideration in conjunction and in comparison with those of the " Older Hands," who have done so much to make the game such a fine and skilful pastime.

AUTHOR'S PREFACE.

" THE Murder of Edwin Drood " has been chosen
as the title of this book because, in the author's
opinion, doubt is no longer possible that Edwin
Drood was murdered. If the intrinsic evidence afforded
by the book, strong as it is, is not thought to be conclusive, yet there remain the added testimonies of Charles
Dickens' son, of his biographer and of his illustrator,
and these render almost inevitable a verdict of " wilful
murder " against John Jasper.

The originality of the story, had Dickens lived to
complete it, was to have consisted in " the review of the
murderer's career by himself at the close, when its
temptations were to be dwelt upon as if not he, the
culprit, but some other man were the tempted." So
Forster tells us in his " Life of Charles Dickens." The last
chapters of the book were to have been written in the condemned cell, and it is for this reason that the present
story takes the form of a manuscript confession by
Jasper of his crime. But since Jasper's wickedness was
to have been " all elaborately elicited from him as if
told of another," the narrative has been framed im-
personally in a series of episodes made to read like a
novel rather than the confession or autobiography of
a murderer. The introductory and the concluding portions, however, are supposed to have been penned in the
first person by Jasper in his condemned cell. These
portions are in fact taken (with such slight adaptations

as the purpose for which they are borrowed renders necessary) from the short story which Dickens named " A confession found in a prison in the time of Charles the Second." This little read story appears in " Master Humphrey's Clock." It is not perhaps a perfect tale, but certainly it is a " strong " one. It tells the story of the murder by an uncle of his brother's child aged four or five. The body was unearthed by bloodhounds from its grave beneath the chair the cowering murderer was then seated upon. After condemnation the murderer reviews his own career and (speaking posthumously from his prison cell) sets down on paper a critical analysis of his morbid mind and motives. The author has ventured to draw upon this story to supply the atmosphere of a Confession such as Dickens had intended to elicit from Jasper.

An apology is no doubt expected from the author for this addition to the already astounding library of books on Edwin Drood. He will also, perhaps, be expected to explain what kind of book it is that he has attempted to achieve. Is it a sequel or a solution ? Continuations and sequels, Mr. Cuming Walters has said, must be sharply distinguished from theories and solutions. The writers of sequels, he has truly added, have " cut the Gordian knot rather than untied it." The solutionists, on the other hand, have honestly attempted extrication. If the author must be classified with one of these, he naturally prefers penning as a sheep with the solutionists to casting forth from the fold with the continuation goats. His claim to be a sheep is that he has honestly attempted extrication of some among the many mysteries of Edwin Drood. He makes no claim to have completed the masterpiece which Charles Dickens of immortal memory has left unfinished. Only the unknown sculptor of the famous Venus could complete that statue *as a work of art.* But a very sorry artist might have the luck to solve the mysteries of its complete construction and by means of a conjecturally completed statue would best convey the original artist's notion.

Good wine needs no bush, and no apology is needed for publishing unpublished words of Dickens. The manuscript of Edwin Drood is in the Forster collection at the Victoria and Albert Museum, South Kensington, and is open to public inspection. Just before the war it occurred to the present author to study this manuscript minutely. He was rewarded by the discovery of passages unmistakably written by Dickens which have never appeared in print. He has transcribed these passages. They will be found incorporated and duly noted in this book. He also scrutinized very carefully for clues, the " Plans " for Edwin Drood that Dickens jotted for his personal use and studied microscopically such of the alterations, deletions and interlineations in the manuscript and proofs as are decipherable. These new discoveries proved of value and one excision in particular threw out a hint by which the author has been enabled as he believes, to solve a mystery that has baffled other solvers. It concerns the quick-lime. (*See App. IV*).

Cloisterham, as the student of the Mystery is of course aware, is Rochester. There was no spire in those days, but otherwise the Cathedral and its precincts have changed but little since the night when Jasper looked down from the Cathedral Tower " on Cloisterham fair to see in the moonlight; its ruined habitations and sanctuaries of the dead at the Tower's base; its moss-softened red tiled roofs and red-brick houses of the living clustering beyond; its river winding down from the mist on the horizon, as though that were its source, and already heaving with a restless knowledge of its approach towards the sea." Like Jasper we are privileged to view this scene; but by daylight and from a point of vantage higher even than the tower top. Sailing high above the City in a sea-plane the camera's uncanny eye unrolls the picture like a map beneath us. Then falling to 800 feet we view the scene as Jasper saw it, but without the tower's obstruction which blocked the view behind him. There, spread out before us, is the whole scene of the murder and the journey Jasper was engaged upon. Next, coming very low we get a splendid view of the graves in one of which was Edwin's " final destination "; and can follow too the route which Jasper took to carry quick-lime to it ; after which we skim the leaded roofs which Jasper scrambled over and fly back to the sea-plane station on the river.

To Major Sippe, D.S.O., of Short Bros., Ltd., the author tenders his most grateful thanks for these air photographs of Rochester. Without them it would have been impossible to convey that local knowledge which is essential to a true understanding of the Mystery. They were taken expressly for this book by a " Short " sea-plane on the 23rd of March, in response to a simple telephone enquiry by the author's friend Mr. C. G. Grey, the Editor of *The Aeroplane,* and quite gratuitously. The author thanks and congratulates the pilot, Mr. Vance E. Galloway, and the photographic staff of Short Bros., Ltd., most heartily.

" There seem to be tens of thousands of persons in this country " (writes a hostile critic of " this eternal controversy ") " who worry over the Drood problem as chess enthusiasts do over mates in five moves.' The accusation is a true one and need not have been limited to this country. But why should we not ? Is it not " an amiable hobby that shies at nothing and kicks nobody ? " Might not we ten thousand have been worse employed ? " Yes, but it leads nowhere," the critic answers " the Mystery is insoluble and the solutionists merely contradict each other." That accusation is not true. Step by step the many mysteries are being solved. The greatest danger is lest the game one day should have an end in a complete solution. But that day is not yet. To his mentors in this game the author tenders thanks for the pleasure he has had from it. He would name especially Professor Henry Jackson (*About Edwin Drood*), Mr. Montagu Saunders (*The Mystery in the Drood Family*), and Mr. Cuming Walters (*The Complete Edwin Drood*). Of Mr. G. F. Gadd (*The Case for Tartar*) the author's temptation is to say " *pereant qui ante nos nostra,*" *etc.*

Besides these and others, the author has received welcome assistance from his brother Major E. D. Carden, who enlarged and adapted for him the Ordnance Map of

B

Rochester, and in a very special degree from Mr. B. W. Matz, but for whose approval, encouragement and assistance, this book would not have been published.

THE MANUSCRIPT BEGINS.

THE MURDER OF
EDWIN DROOD

THE MANUSCRIPT BEGINS.

THIS is the last night I have to live, and I will set down the naked truth without disguise. I am a double murderer.

I was never a cheerful or a happy man. From childhood I have always been of a solemn, sombre, secret nature.

I speak of myself as if I had passed from the world, for while I write this, my grave is digging and my name is written in the black book of death.

I had a nephew—Ned. I say " I had," because last Christmas Eve I killed and buried him. In the prim prison cemetery outside this cell, I hear my burial preparing. Ned never heard my preparation of his place of sepulture. To-morrow as I travel to the scaffold through the cemetery I shall see my open grave. To think how often Ned and I have gone together through that other churchyard and passed his burying place ; two fellow-travellers [1] on the road of death ! To think how many

---

[1] *Two Fellow Travellers.* The phrase " a fellow-traveller," employed by Jasper, in the opium den, of Edwin, has evoked discussion. Some read it literally, others in a sense merely metaphorical. Jasper and Edwin had travelled together literally and often past the latter's destined grave unknown to Edwin. Metaphorically, too, the pair were fellow-travellers on the road of death and neither knew it. The ambiguity is probably intentional.

times he went the journey and never saw the road !
Ned never knew his death was near.   He died without
a struggle.

Perhaps I hide the truth from myself, but I do not
think that when this began I meditated to do him any
wrong.   I may have thought how serviceable his in-
heritance would be to me, and may have wished him
dead ; but I believe I had no thought of compassing his
death.   Neither did the idea come upon me at once,
but by very slow degrees, presenting itself at first in
very dim shapes at a very great distance, as men may
think of an earthquake or the last day ; then drawing
nearer and nearer, and losing something of its horror
and improbability ; then coming to be part and parcel
—nay nearly the whole sum and substance—of my daily
thoughts, and resolving itself into a question of means
and safety ; not of doing or abstaining from the deed.
While this was going on within me I never could bear
that Ned should call me Uncle ; nor have him note the
intentness of my look—that look of hungry, exacting,
watchful and yet (as he supposed) devoted affection
which I knew to be always on my face when addressed
in his direction.   And yet I was under a fascination
which made it a kind of business with me to contemplate
his slight and fragile figure and think how easily it
might be done.   Sometimes I would steal upstairs and
watch him as he slept.[2]   How easy it would be to smother
him !

[2] *As he slept.* "His nephew lies asleep, calm and untroubled.
John Jasper stands looking down upon him, his unlighted pipe in his
hand, for a long time with a fixed attention."

" Inhuman callous brute," I hear you call me,
" cold-bloodedly to set down thus the morbid details
of his murderous thoughts and actions."

No longer, therefore, will I tell my tale myself ;
but will set forth instead the story of another murderer.

EPISODE I.

DEAD AND BURIED.

College Gate.
(or Chertsey's Gate)
Rochester.

JOHN JASPER'S GATEWAY.

EPISODE I.

DEAD AND BURIED.

ON the Eve of Christmas, 1842, at midnight precisely, and at the very climax of the great storm which went thundering along the empty streets rattling at all the latches and tearing at all the shutters as if warning the people to get up and fly with it, John Jasper murdered Edwin Drood.

Jealousy was the motive of the murder and a large black scarf of strong close-woven silk the instrument. The death was instantaneous [1]; the body hidden immediately.[2]

Staged at Cloisterham, the tragedy took place within the sombre precincts of the old Cathedral. Among these secluded nooks there is very little stir or movement after dark. There is little enough in the high tide of the day, but there is next to none at night. Besides that the cheerfully frequented High Street is the natural channel in which the Cloisterham traffic flows, a certain awful hush pervades the ancient pile, the cloisters and the churchyard after dark which not many people care

---

[1] *The Death was Instantaneous.* Jasper tells the Opium Woman as much. " Time and place are both at hand. . . Hush! The journey's made. Its over." " So soon ? " " That's what I said to you. So soon."

[2] *The Body Hidden Immediately.* The site of the murder and of the burial must have been close together. Common sense requires it. Also Forster says so. " By means of a gold ring which had resisted the corrosive effects of the lime into which he had thrown the body, not only the person murdered was to have been identified, but the locality of the crime."

to encounter. One might fancy that the tide of life
was stemmed by Mr. Jasper's own Gatehouse. The
murmur of the tide is heard beyond. But no wave
passes the archway over which his lamp burns red
behind his curtain as if the building were a lighthouse.

On this Christmas Eve, three are to dine together
in the house of Jasper on the margin of the tide of life.
The host is to be peacemaker between his nephew and
the shy fierce stranger Neville Landless, with whom
Edwin has quarrelled bitterly. A social dinner and the
season of good-will provide the occasion. Neville is
the first to arrive at the postern stair beneath the gateway. Twice he passes it by, reluctant it seems to enter.
" I wish I were not going to this dinner; Helena," he
has told his sister. But at last with a rapid turn, he
passes in.

Edwin Drood comes next. He has spent a solitary
day, and as he strolls about and about to pass the time
until the dinner hour, his wonted carelessness has been
replaced by a wistful looking at and dwelling upon all
the familiar landmarks of Cloisterham. He will soon
be far away and may never see them again, he thinks.
Ah, he little knows [3] how near a case he has for thinking
so. Poor youth, poor youth ! The Cathedral chime
strikes a sudden surprise to his heart as he turns in under
the archway of the Gatehouse. And so *he* goes up the
postern stair.

John Jasper passes a more agreeable and cheerful

---

[3] *He little knows.* This passage is here published for the first time
from Dickens' manuscript (see Author's Introduction). " Poor
youth, poor youth ! " was substituted in the printed book.

day than either of his guests. He is in beautiful voice this day. In the pathetic supplication to have his heart inclined to keep this law he quite astonishes his fellows by his melodious power. His nervous temperament is occasionally prone to take difficult music a little too quickly. To-day his time is perfect. These results are probably attained by a grand composure of the spirits. The mere mechanism of his throat is a little tender for he wears a large black scarf of strong close-woven silk slung loosely round his neck. After service he accompanies Mr. Crisparkle to Minor Canon Corner to call for Neville. Finding that his guest has already left for the Gatehouse, he bids good-night to the Minor Canon on the latter's doorstep, retraces his steps to the Cathedral door, and turns down past it towards his home. He sings in a low voice and with delicate expression as he walks along. It still seems as if a false note were not in his power to-night, and as if nothing could hurry or retard him. Arriving thus under the arched entrance of his dwelling, he pauses for an instant in the shelter to pull off that great black scarf, and hang it in a loop upon his arm. For that brief time his face is knitted and stern. But it immediately clears, as he resumes his singing and his way. And so *he* goes up the postern stair.

" Three are to meet at the Gatehouse to-night."

They meet and dine and the dinner is dull but decorous. The quarrel is healed and some half-hour before midnight the dinner party breaks up.

At Jasper's suggestion Neville and Edwin go down to the river to see the action of the wind there. Jasper

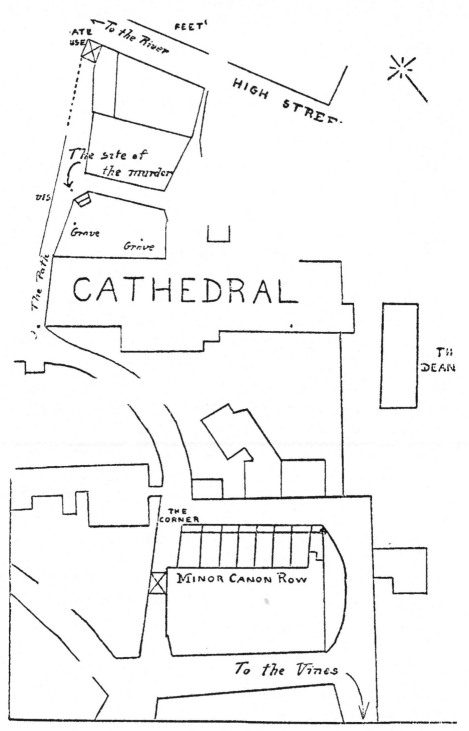

BASED UPON THE ORDNANCE SURVEY MAP WITH THE SANC
OF THE CONTROLLER OF H.M. STATIONERY OFFICE.

excuses himself on the score of his throat and bids them good-night at the foot of the postern stair.

> " When shall these three meet again ?
> In thunder, lightning or in rain ? "

.   No sooner have the pair turned down the High Street towards the river than Jasper regains his room, · changes his coat for a pea-jacket, puts on his low-crowned flap-brimmed hat, loops once more upon his arm the black silk scarf, and treading softly down the postern stair, issues forth carrying keys and an unlit lantern. He turns right-handed [4] towards the churchyard and cathedral, and leaves the High Street and his guests behind him.   On reaching the railed-in graveyard on his left he unlocks the gate and steps inside.   Then selecting a vault and entering it, he comes out again almost at once, leaving his unlit lamp within.   He then pursues the path past the west door of the cathedral.   This brings him to Minor Canon Row, at the end of which farthest from Neville's temporary home there is a piece of old dwarf wall, breast high, the only remaining boundary of what was once a garden, but is now the thoroughfare.

---

[4] *He turns Right-handed.*   The reader is invited to consult the plan and the air photographs from time to time for explanation and confirmation of the story.   Turning sharp to the left on coming out of the west door of the Cathedral, the only path leads straight to Minor Canon Corner, which is at the west end of an obvious row of houses. This path continued leads to " the Vines " (not in the picture).   Returning past the West Door, the path bisects the cemetery.   The Drood sarcophagus and Sapsea tomb are in the right-hand, darkly shadowed portion of the graveyard.   In the nearer photographic view the gate posts of the entrance to this part can just be seen. Next comes a church, and after that the Gatehouse spanning the footway " on the margin of the tide of life," with the High Street visible beyond it.

Behind this old dwarf wall Jasper stops and takes his
station. Folding his arms upon the top of the wall
he rests his chin on them and waits and watches.

Meanwhile the storm blows and abates not. No
such power of wind has blown for many a winter night.
Chimneys topple in the streets and Neville and Edwin
hold to posts and corners and to one another to keep
themselves upon their feet. At last they reach the
Corner, and take slight shelter from the storm beneath
the porch above the Minor Canon's doorstep.[5] As
they part amicably, standing in the shaft of light cast
through the open door from within the house, Jasper sees
and watches them. This is the final meeting, and two
of the three part there for ever. The door closes on Neville.
Edwin retraces his steps towards the Gatehouse and so
to bed. Cat-like, Jasper follows him. They pass the
great West door of the Cathedral in close succession
following the path across the pitch dark precincts.
As the Cathedral tower tolls midnight they approach
the steps which lead through the unlocked gate in the
railings into the burial ground. Unheard in the echoing
sounds Jasper closes in with sudden move upon his
devoted victim and in an instant the great black scarf
is tight round Edwin's windpipe. Without a struggle,
an entreaty, without any consciousness of peril, Edwin is
dead.

" Time and Place are both at hand." Time—midnight, Christmas Eve at the height of the great storm.

[5] *The Porch above the Minor Canon's Doorstep.*   All the houses
in the Row have porches.   " They had odd little porches over the doors
like sounding-boards over old pulpits."

Place—the dark Cathedral Precincts. " Time, Place and Fellow Traveller." At midnight, on the eve of Christmas, at the point of greatest fury of the storm, crossing the deserted graveyard homeward bound goes Edwin Drood. " Hush," softly behind him Jasper approaches. " The journey's made, it's over." Ned is dead. " Wait ·a little. This is a vision. I shall sleep it off. It has been too short and easy. I must have a better vision than this ; this is the poorest of all. No struggle, no consciousness of peril, no en-treaty." Jasper in a sort of daze, between sleeping and waking stands over his victim half believing that he dreams it all.

" And yet I never saw that before ! " Jasper is startled out of this reverie by his glance having fallen upon the corpse still lying at his feet. " Look at it ! Look what a poor mean miserable thing it is ! [6] . *That* must be real. It's over." He knows his dream for reality at last. For the first time, too, he discovers the insignificance and weakness of that formidable and dangerous obstacle (as up to now he has pictured his rival to himself) the removal of which from his path he has made the one object of his life.

With the realization there comes with a rush the need for instant action to conceal his crime. It is the work of less than a minute for Jasper to lift the body

[6] *Look what a poor mean miserable thing it is !* Compare with this passage *The Dream of Eugene Aram.*
" Two sudden blows with a ragged stick and one with a heavy stone.
One hurried gash with a hasty knife—and then the deed was done !
There was nothing lying at my feet but lifeless flesh and bone.
Nothing but lifeless flesh and bone that could not do me ill."

in his arms, carry it up the two steps into the burial
ground and lay it on the grass for one moment outside
the sarcophagus within which lies the poor lad's final
destination.[7] A few moments more are occupied in
opening the door of the tomb, closing it again behind
them, and lighting the lantern within. Its dim light
discloses a spade, a small heap of lime and a cavity laid
bare by the removal of a few bricks from the wall.
What are these things doing here ? Jasper has a last
precaution to be taken before that appears. Kneeling
by the body he takes from its clothing all articles of
jewellery[8] which he knows to be there. They are a watch
and chain and shirt pin. This done he lifts the body
into the cavity, then covers it completely with quick-
lime and walls it up with bricks and mortar. Ned is
hidden as safely as though buried in the Pyramids he
tells himself ! Nothing now remains but to dust from
his clothing all specks of lime, extinguish the lantern,
open the door of the sarcophagus, close it and lock it

[7] *The Sarcophagus. . . the Final Destination.* During a lover's
quarrel Edwin refers to " my destination " whereupon Rosa takes
him up " you are not going to be buried in the Pyramids I hope ? "
Previous investigators have generally assumed that if Edwin's destination was a tomb, that tomb was Mrs. Sapsea's. The present author
prefers to place him in the Drood sarcophagus. The Drood family
tomb, which lay close to Mrs. Sapsea's, seems somehow more appro-
priate than her's—an utter stranger. Jasper, as the elder Drood's
executor, no doubt would be the person to have the key of his sarcophagus. There is, however, no evidence that the cavity was in this
particular tomb—it was not in Mrs. Sapsea's.

[8] *Edwin's Jewellery.* " He (Jasper) said with a smile that he had
an inventory in his mind of all the jewellery his gentleman relative ever
wore ; namely his watch and chain and his shirt pin." The original
of the watchmaker to whom Jasper made this remark seems to have
been D'Oiley the watchmaker in " The Disappearance of John
Acland."

behind him, and return, noiseless and alone, to the lonely Gatehouse where the steady light is burning.

That was Ned's last Christmas Eve.

EPISODE II.

A KEY AND ITS KEEPER.

EPISODE II.

A KEY AND ITS KEEPER.

MR. Thomas Sapsea, auctioneer, having invited Mr. John Jasper, Lay Precentor and Choir Master of Rochester Cathedral to supper at Mr. Sapsea's house in the High Street on a day in the late Autumn before November 9th,[1] receives him there in his ground floor sitting-room characteristically attended by his portrait, his eight-day clock and his weather-glass. Durdles, stonemason, also looks in by invitation to take a glass of port with them and to receive instructions from Mr. Sapsea anent an inscription to be placed upon the late Mrs. Sapsea's funeral monument.

Mrs. Sapsea's key is about to go into an inner breast pocket of Durdle's flannel coat when Jasper interrupts with a remark which leads to this key, and two others, being handed to him to feel their weight. Improvising conversation with Durdles the while, Jasper not only feels the weight of the keys but also studies the Sapsea key with .care, mentally noting the feel of its wards and the tone it gives out when struck. Then with ingenuous and friendly face he hands them back to Durdles who departs leaving Jasper and Sapsea to a hit at backgammon, followed by a supper of cold

---

[1] *Before November 9th.* At this meeting with Jasper, Mr. Sapsea is not yet Mayor of Rochester. His importance has received this enhancement by the night of the unaccountable expedition. Lord Mayor's Day (November 9th), has therefore intervened.

roast beef and salad. It is to be observed that the
Sapsea key is not returned, as are the other two, into an
inner pocket but is tied up in the dinner bundle, without
which Durdles never appears in public.

On Monday, November 14th,[2] Jasper is again
present at a little party. This is the friendly dinner of
eight at Minor Canon Corner, planned by Mr. Crisparkle,
and utterly spoilt by Honeythunder, the ninth and
uninvited guest. Disasters succeed one another throughout the evening and culminate in the quarrel at the Gatehouse. Neville goes home hatless and, Edwin having gone
to bed, Jasper follows Neville, with his hat, for the double
purpose of assuring himself that the boy has really gone
back to his tutor's and has not drowned himself, or done
anything equally fatal to Jasper's plans and of blackening
the case against him to Mr. Crisparkle without raising
suspicion as to his own motives. These benevolent
aims accomplished, Jasper returns home through the
Close,[3] but on his way is brought to a standstill by the
spectacle of Stony Durdles, dinner bundle and all,

[2] *Monday, November 14th.* This date is arbitrary except that
it was a Monday "so many weeks" before Friday, December 16th,
the day of the wonderful closet.

[3] *Returns home through the Close.* See the Note *The Late Commotion*
on page 25.

Professor Jackson gives a full account of the transposition of
chapter V in "About Edwin Drood," and the author adopts his views
verbatim. In addition to the evidence he puts forward it should be mentioned (1) That the way from Sapsea's to the Gatehouse is *not* "through
the Close," (2) That the manuscript comment on the Sapsea monument introduced by Durdles is "with inscription finished." This
is impossible if the same night as that in which it was put in hand is
intended and (3) That the manuscript reference to "glittering fragments of the late commotion" is meaningless unless the night of
Neville's quarrel is the night in question.

leaning against the railing of the burial ground while
Deputy flings stones at him in the moonlight.

This chance meeting with Durdles, in this state, is
most opportune for Jasper's plans. Offering to accom-
pany Durdles to his home, Jasper first ascertains that
the all-important key still lies where last he saw it put.
This he does by patting the dinner bundle and hearing
the key clink. Next he tries to secure possession of
the bundle[4] for a moment, but Durdles will not part
with it, but starts, instead, to introduce to Jasper,
in drunken fashion, the gravestones near-by[5] beginning
with " Your own brother-in-law," and not forgetting
Mrs. Sapsea, that devoted wife whose tomb now dis-
plays the famous inscription finished.[6] To have him on
his own ground,[7] while helping him along, Jasper asks
Durdles about his ramblings in the Crypt and round
about the Cathedral, and gets Durdles to agree to let
him go about with him sometime on these strange ex-
peditions of his among the tombs, vaults, towers and
ruins. As the mental state of Durdles[8] and of all his
sodden tribe is one hardly susceptible of astonishment

[4] *Shall I carry your bundle?* Manuscript adds " Jasper pats it
and it clinks," also " ' Not on any account,' repeats Durdles, adjusting
it."

[5] *The Gravestones Near-by.* The manuscript has " Introducing a
distant Sarchophagus," written and then deleted.

[6] *With Inscription Finished*, manuscript. " Departed Assessed
Taxes " was " Departed King's Taxes," and the gravestone of the
much respected muffin-maker was " With extinguished torch."

[7] *To have him on his own ground.* There words are in the manuscript immediately following " Is there anything new down in the
Crypt, Durdles ? " asks John Jasper.

[8] *The Mental State of Durdles.* The whole of this passage is from
the manuscript.

in itself so it is one hardly susceptible of any reasonable interpretation by other minds. But it happens to fall out to-night—just as it might have happened to fall out quite the other way—that Durdles rather likes his position in the dialogue and chuckles over it.

When Jasper, pursuing his subject of romantic interest, says that what he dwells upon most is the remarkable accuracy with which Durdles would seem to find out where people are buried, Durdles decides to demonstrate his skill and looks about for some ledge or corner to place his bundle on. Jasper is quick to seize his chance and relieve him of it. Clink, clink. And his hammer is handed him. The Sapsea key is still within the bundle. How does Jasper know this? He is used to pitching his note by sounding for it.[9] At Sapsea's house he memorized the note the key gives out, and now " clink, clink " he has heard the note he seeks. Clearly the key has its regular residence tied up in the bundle where Jasper is content to leave it until he needs it.

Deputy is now given warning and paid his wages and the longish journey is resumed. They have but to cross the Vines to come into Crow Lane at the bottom of which stands the crazy wooden house, the Traveller's Twopenny.[10] As Jasper and Durdles come near this place a woman is seen [11] crouching and smoking in the cold night air on a seat just outside the door which

[9] *By sounding for it.* Manuscript. " You pitch your note by sounding for it, don't you Mr. Jasper ? "

[10] *The Traveller's Twopenny.* It is not without interest that this famous spot was nearly called " The Traveller's Threepenny Lodgings." The manuscript has it so with Threepenny deleted.

[11] See next page.

stands ajar. Of a sudden Jasper stops and looks at this woman—the lighter coloured figure of Durdles being between himself ᵗand her—very keenly. " Is that Deputy " ? she croaks out in a whimpering and feeble way ; " where have you been you young good-for- nothing wretch ? " " Out for my 'elth " returns the hideous sprite. " I'll claw you," retorts the woman, " when I can lay my fingers on you. I'll be bad for your 'elth (O me, O me, my breath is so short), I wanted my pipe and my little spoon and ye'd been and put 'em on a shelf I couldn't find." " Wot did yer go to bed for then," retorts Deputy quite unabashed. " Who'd ha' thought you was going to get up again ? " " You, you might ha' known I was like to do it." " Yer lie," says Deputy in his only form of contradiction.[11] Further wrangling between the two is stopped by some half- dozen other hideous small boys who start into the moon- light like vultures attracted by some carrion scent of Deputy in the air, and instantly fall to stoning him and one another. Durdles remarks of the young savages with some point that " They haven't got an object " and leads the way down the lane. At the junction of Crow Lane with the High Street, they turn the corner into safety [12] and Jasper takes Durdles home—Durdles stumbling up his stony yard [13] as if he were going to

[11] *A Woman is seen. . . His only form of contradiction.* The whole of this passage is in the manuscript verbatim. Its exclusion from the printed book is explained by a Note in the manuscript headed " Plans."

[12] *They turn the corner into safety.* This is clearly the corner formed by the junction of Crow Lane and the High Street.

[13] See next page.

turn headforemost into one of the unfinished tombs. John Jasper returns to his Gatehouse by another way [14] —the High Street—and entering softly with his key, finds his fire still burning and on the hearth some glittering fragments of the late commotion [15] He ascends an inner staircase of only a few steps leading to two rooms. One his own sleeping chamber, one his nephew's.[16] There is a light in each. His nephew lies asleep, calm and untroubled. Jasper stands looking down upon him a long time with a fixed attention. Then he passes to his own room, lights his pipe of opium and delivers himself to the ghosts and phantoms it invokes at midnight. So ends this long eventful Monday.

[13] *Up his stony yard.* " Up " in the manuscript becomes " among the litter of " in the printed text. The ground in fact runs uphill on that side of the High Street.

[14] *Another way.* See the plan. Observe how carefully Dickens leads the reader on to the conclusion that Durdle's house is far away from the cemetery; as it is by any orthodox approach. Compare also : " We can't help going round by the Traveller's Twopenny, if we go the short way, which is the back way." The manuscript has " we must go "and " the right way " both deleted. It is not accidental.

[15] *The Late Commotion.* This is from the manuscript. It proves to the hilt Professor Jackson's theory of the displacement of Chapter V.

[16] *One his Own. . . One his Nephew's.* The verbal deviations from the printed text here are taken from the manuscript.

EPISODE III.

ACCOUNTS FOR THE UNACCOUNTABLE.

EPISODE III.

ACCOUNTS FOR THE UNACCOUNTABLE.[1]

MONDAY, December 19th [2] the third day after Mr. Crisparkle's mission of peace to Jasper, brings a letter from Edwin,[3] proposing (as Jasper had advised him to propose) a friendly dinner with Neville on Xmas Eve " the better the day the better the deed, and let there be only we three, and let us shake hands all round there and then, and say no more about it." The date fixed for the dinner is less than a week ahead. So Jasper takes the letter round at once to the Minor Canon, who, quite elated, asks " You expect Mr. Neville, then," to which Jasper's reply is " I count upon his coming." On the evening of the same day Mr. Sapsea, now Mayor of Rochester, is walking slowly with his

[1] *The Unaccountable Expedition.* This chapter according to the manuscript " Plans," was to " lay the ground for the manner of the murder to come out at last." Unless the murder really was a murder it is difficult to see how the manner of it could come out at last !

[2] *Monday, December* 19th. Mr. Crisparkle fixes this date by what he says to Neville (*see below*). The group which met in view of the Gatehouse on this Monday evening has been placed by Sir L. Fildes, in his striking illustration, on the exact spot chosen by Jasper for the murder of his nephew. It was not, however, where Sapsea stands at the entrance to the left-hand portion of the graveyard that Jasper throttled Edwin, but just behind the cautioning figure of Durdles whose back is turned on his own yard. Jasper, who is looking at Durdles, can see beyond him a corner entrance to the larger piece of burial ground containing the Sapsea tomb and Drood sarcophagus. The Dean's field of vision includes another pathway along which at a later hour to-night Jasper will be carrying quick-lime from Durdles' yard towards Edwin's burial place (*see the plan*).

[3] *Edwin's Letter.* Immediately he learnt from Neville on the previous Friday of Neville's infatuation for Rosa, Mr. Crisparkle had

hands behind him near the Churchyard. Turning a
corner he comes at once into the goodly presence of the
Dean conversing with the Verger and Mr. Jasper about
Jasper's nocturnal expedition to be made to-night with
Durdles. Sapsea appearing thus opportunely, Jasper
makes prompt use of the pompous ass by naming him

exacted pledges from him (a) not to divulge his secret to Rosa, and
(b) that Drood making the first advance the quarrel between them
should be ended for ever. To secure that Drood shall make the first
advance, Crisparkle decides to seek the aid of Jasper, to whom he
says "I want to establish peace between these two young fellows,"
Jasper is perplexed. No wonder. The quarrel is essential to his
scheme, and yet he must appear to wish to bring about a reconciliation.
"How?" he asked. "I want you to get your nephew to write you
a short note in his lively fashion saying that he is willing to shake hands."
Jasper turned that perplexed face towards the fire. Mr. Crisparkle
found it even more perplexing than before, inasmuch as it seemed
to denote (which could hardly be) some close internal calculation."
    Jasper was calculating—was there time? There was less than
a week to Christmas. Edwin would arrive on the 23rd to make the
final preparation for the marriage. He still might break off the engagement and live. He must be given until Christmas Eve at least. Yet
a reconciliation with Neville could not be long postponed if once they
met each other, as they were bound to do in Cloisterham. A public
notorious reconciliation would be fatal to Jasper's plans. Why not
a private one, with no witnesses, on Christmas Eve, immediately before
the time fixed by Jasper for the murder? That would bring the two
together at the vital moment for Jasper's plans. Rightly regarded,
in fact, this suggestion of Mr. Crisparkle's will smooth the way for
Jasper's plan (manuscript "plans" has noted against the title of the
Chapter "Smoothing the Way," that is for Jasper's plan through Mr.
Crisparkle who takes new ground on Neville's new confidence.) Yes,
but will Neville come? Is it safe to rely on his coming? "You are
always responsible and trustworthy Mr. Crisparkle. Do you really
feel sure that you can answer for Neville so confidently?" "I do."
The perplexed and perplexing look vanished. "I will do it." As
soon as Mr. Crisparkle had left him, Jasper sat down and drafted
and sent to Edwin the letter he wished to receive from him. Thus
making it appear as if his own suggested time table originated with
Edwin. On the third day after this (Sunday intervening), he received
from Edwin the letter for which he had asked containing nothing
altered or added except expressions of affection and a postscript.

as the real originator of his own odd archæological whim ; Jasper even succeeds in causing Sapsea to say that he himself recollects having made the suggestion ! Durdles then comes slouching up and he too joins the group and amuses the others by cautioning Sapsea against the bad habit of boasting ; after which caution Sapsea stalks off. Durdles then going home to clean himself, the group breaks up ; the Dean withdrawing to his dinner, Tope to his tea, and Jasper to his piano where he sits chanting choir music in a low voice until it has been for some time dark and the moon is about to rise. Then he closes his piano softly, softly changes his coat for a pea jacket, with a goodly wicker-cased bottle in its largest pocket and putting on a low-crowned flap-brimmed hat goes softly out.

Why does he move so softly to-night ? No outward reason is apparent for it. Can there be any sympathetic reason crouching darkly within him ?

Jasper next repairs, as arranged, to Durdles' home. Durdles is an old bachelor, and he lives in a little antiquated hole of a house that was never finished ; supposed to be built so far of stones stolen from the City wall. It overlooks the Churchyard.[4] To this abode there is an approach ankle deep in stone chips.

---

[4] *It overlooks the Churchyard.* These words are omitted in the printed book. In the manuscript they form part of the description of Durdles' home given in Chapter IV. They solve a problem of great importance. They explain how it was possible for Jasper to carry the quick-lime from Durdles' yard to the Drood sarcophagus without attracting observation. (*See Appendix IV*). The exact position of Durdles' yard is therefore of great importance. It is clearly shewn upon the plan.

D

Turning in here from the High Street, Jasper finds Durdles ready for their unaccountable expedition. Durdles takes his dinner bundle, a lantern and some matches and they start out together. Jasper, who is ahead at the yard gate, is warned by Durdles to beware of the mound of lime he sees there " quick enough to eat your boots. With a little handy stirring quick enough to eat your bones." But it is not Jasper's bones which are destined to that fate and so they go on towards the Cathedral presently passing the red windows of the Traveller's Twopenny and emerging into the clear moonlight of the Monk's Vineyard. This crossed they come to Minor Canon Row of which the greater part lies in shadow until the moon [5] shall rise higher in the sky.

The sound of a closing house door strikes their ears, and two men come out. They are Mr. Crisparkle and Neville. Jasper with a strange and sudden smile upon his face lays the palm of his hand upon the breast of Durdles stopping him where he stands.

[5] *The Moon.* Careful attention is devoted by Dickens (and should be by the reader) to the moonlight shadows throughout the evening. The references to them are part of the plot, and not merely padding or picturesqueness. By a happy coincidence the shadows cast by the sun when the air photograph was being taken approximate very closely indeed to those cast by the moon on the night in question.

Jasper sat at his piano with no light but that of the fire from early dusk, " for two or three hours, in short, until it has been for some time dark, and the moon is about to rise." The sun set that night at 3·50, and the moon rose two hours and five minutes later. The moon, by the way, was at the full two nights before this. It seems, therefore, that the start of the expedition was about 7 p.m., and that it lasted some six hours or more.

At that end of Minor Canon Row, the shadow is profound in the existing state of the light; at that end too there is a piece of old dwarf wall [6] breast high, the only remaining boundary of what was once a garden but is now the thoroughfare. Jasper and Durdles would have turned this wall in another instant, but stopping so, short, stand behind it.

" These two are only sauntering," Jasper whispers, " they will go out into the moonlight soon. Let us keep quiet here or they will detain us or want to join us, or what not."

Durdles nods assent and falls to munching some fragments from his bundle. Jasper folds his arms upon the top of the wall and with his chin resting on them, watches Neville as though his eye were at the trigger [7] of a loaded rifle, and he had covered him and were going to fire. A sense of destructive power is so expressed in his face that even Durdles pauses in his munching and looks at him with an unmunched something in his cheek.

Meanwhile Mr. Crisparkle and Neville walk to and fro quietly talking together. What they say [8] cannot

[6] *A piece of old dwarf wall.* Some such piece of wall is shewn on a large scale plan by Mr. St. John Hope, which the writer has seen in the British Museum. This is the wall from behind which Jasper watches the final parting between Neville and Edwin. It is at the east end of Minor Canon Row and is indicated by a small black spot upon the plan. (*See Episode I*).

[7] *Eye . . at the trigger.* We small fry like to catch the giants tripping ! Compare with this Rosa's " dark bright pouting eye " in Chapter III.

[8] *What they say.* Crisparkle is telling Neville about his interview with Jasper three days before and of the letter from Edwin just received, Neville feels himself morally bound to go to the dinner, bearing in mind his pledge and Mr. Crisparkle's reminder " Remember that I said I answered for you confidently." He agrees to go.

be heard consecutively, but Mr. Jasper has already distinguished his own name more than once.

" This is the first day of the week," Mr. Crisparkle can be distinctly heard to observe as they turn back " and the last day of the week is Christmas Eve."

" You may be certain of me, Sir."

The echoes were favourable at those points and Jasper knows from Neville's own lips that Neville can be counted on ; that, however unwillingly, he will come to the Gatehouse dinner. The pair slowly disappear, passing out into the moonlight at the other end of Minor Canon Row.[9] It is not until they are gone that Mr. Jasper moves, but then he turns to Durdles and bursts into a fit of laughter.

Before descending into the crypt by the small north door [10] of which Durdles has the key, Jasper scrutinizes the whole expanse of moonlit churchyard in his view, and finds it utterly deserted. One might fancy that the tide of life was stemmed by his own Gatehouse. The murmur of the tide is heard beyond; but no wave passes the archway over which his lamp burns red [11] behind the curtain, as if the building were a Lighthouse. Even in moonlight the churchyard is deserted.

[9] *The other end of Minor Canon Row.* The pair must have gone through the Prior's gate else they would meet Durdles and Jasper later on their journey. The site of the Prior's gate is shewn upon the plan and in Kitton's drawing of it (*see the frontispiece*), in which the chimneys of Mr. Crisparkle's house are seen beyond.

[10] *North Door.* The crypt must have been entered from the North side or Jasper's gatehouse would not have been in view. The point is of some importance since Durdles' yard is on the north.

[11] *Lamp Burns Red.* Jasper is in the habit of leaving his lamp burning although he is out. It is also burning at midnight on Christmas Eve.

They enter, locking themselves in, descend the rugged steps and are down in the Crypt. The taciturnity of Durdles is for the time overcome by the contents of Jasper's wicker bottle [12] of which he partakes freely while Jasper only rinses his mouth once and casts forth the rinsing. So Durdles talks as up and down the lanes of light they walk some little while. They are to ascend the Great Tower. On the steps by which they rise to the Cathedral, Durdles pauses and seats himself upon a step. Mr. Jasper seats himself upon another. The odour from the wicker bottle (which has somehow passed into Durdles keeping) soon intimates that the cork has been taken out. Durdles drinks and drinks and finds it good. He tells his story of his last Christmas Eve, and the ghostly cries [13] he heard and provokes a fierce retort from Jasper who adds " Come we shall freeze here ; lead the way." Durdles complies not over steadily, and seems unconscious of the close scrutiny of Jasper [14] while fumbling among his pockets for a key confided to him [15] that will open an iron gate and so enable them to pass to the staircase of the Great Tower.

[12] *Wicker Bottle.* The contents were " bought on purpose " to make Durdles sleep, whether drugged or merely extra strong who can say ?

[13] *Ghostly Cries.* What is the " ghost " of a sound ? Can it be the " shadow " cast by a sound not yet uttered on the ghostly anniversary before its utterance ? The idea recalls the words that Thomas Campbell found himself repeating as he awoke out of sleep " Coming events cast their shadows before." Anyhow Jasper finds the story a little " creepy " in the chilling crypt.

[14] *The close scrutiny of Jasper.* Jasper watches the influence of the drink on Durdles minutely in order so to time their travels that Durdles shall be overcome when they reach the crypt and when the moon is wholly off the churchyard.

[15] See next page.

"That and the bottle are enough for you to carry," says Jasper, giving the key to Durdles, "hand your bundle to me." Durdles hesitates for a moment be-ween bundle and bottle; but gives the preference to the bottle, and by this simple stratagem, Jasper secures the bundle and the key tied up in it.

Then they go up the winding staircase of the great tower, and at last they look down on Rochester fair to see in the moonlight; its ruined habitations and sanctuaries of the dead at the tower's base. Jasper (always moving softly with no visible reason) contem-plates especially that stillest part which the Cathedral overshadows.[16] But he contemplates Durdles quite as curiously, and Durdles is by times conscious of his watchful eyes. Only by times because Durdles is getting drowsy. On his way down he charges himself with more liquid from the wicker bottle. Durdles who is as seldom drunk as sober is drugged with drink to-night, and when they reach the crypt he half drops, half throws himself down by one of the heavy pillars and is asleep at once, and in his sleep he dreams a dream.[17] He

[15] *Key confided to him.* Perhaps the Dean's permission was necessary for Jasper to have this key whence sprang the earlier con-versation with that functionary. Durdles must have been very fuddled not to notice the absurdity of being handed a key to lighten his load! It is not *that* key that Jasper needs, but the one tied up in Durdles' bundle which he secures by this very simple stratagem without Durdles being aware he has ever parted with it.

[16] *Which the Cathedral overshadows.* At this hour this will be the west and north-west—in other words a portion of the churchyard. It should be noted that the Cathedral is not correctly orientated.

[17] *He dreams a dream.* The dream is his subconscious realisa-tion of what is actually occurring, not a dream unrelated to immediate occurrences.

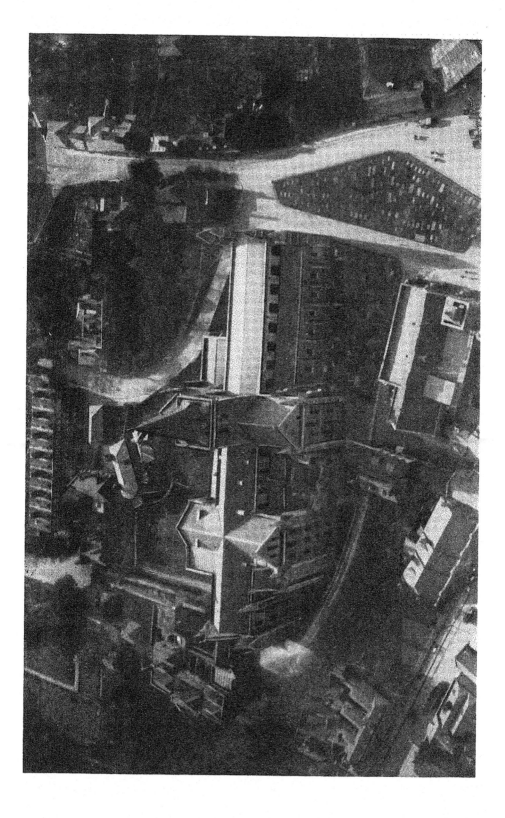

dreams of lying there asleep and yet counting his companion's footsteps as he walks to and fro. He dreams that the footsteps die away into distance of time and space. Actually what takes place meanwhile is this ; Jasper at first walks to and fro with heavy tread. Then hushing his footsteps, softly tip toe, Jasper comes close to Durdles. Durdles dreams that something touches him, and that something falls from his hand. Then something clinks and gropes about. Actually Jasper touches him and the Crypt key falls from his hand, and Jasper gropes about and picks it up. He dreams that he is alone for so long a time that the lanes of light take new directions as the moon advances in her course.[18] Actually he *is* alone this long while. Jasper is gone from the Crypt taking lantern and keys and letting himself out by the same North door by which they entered.

Emerging into the Churchyard, it is no longer moonlit. The southing of the moon has cast the heavy shadow of the nave over the whole expanse of burial ground and churchyard. All is dark and deserted. Still moving softly but quickly, Jasper visits first the Sapsea tomb, opens it with Durdles' key and leaves the lantern within. Then closes but does not lock the door. Next he hastens with noiseless footsteps along the path which leads from the graveyard eastwards, passing beneath an archway and keeping within the shadows cast by the Cathedral until he reaches an angle in the

[18] *The moon advances in her course.* The southing of the moon took place that night a little after one o'clock (1-7 to be precise). The lanes of light would be changing their angle all the time. But the most noticeable change came when they fell through the south windows of the crypt in place of through the north.

wall from the far side of which Durdles' unfinished
dwelling overlooks the Churchyard precincts. The wall
is low and not difficult to pass. Once across it Jasper
finds a spade [19] in Durdles' yard, and making several
journeys, carries sufficient quick lime for his purpose
and heaps it in the churchyard—where? In Mrs.
Sapsea's tomb.[20] When Jasper has collected sufficient
lime within it, and is satisfied that he has not been
observed, he unlocks the Drood sarcophagus with a key
in his possession and transfers the lime to it. Also
the lantern which (having closed the door) he lights.
By its aid and by sounding with the handle of the spade
he finds a hollow portion of the wall, and by removing
a few bricks soon discloses a cavity [21] large enough to
house a body. Into the cavity he drops some quick-
lime and arranges the bricks where he can easily get
at them to put them back. The lime not yet required is
heaped at the further end of the tomb away from the

[19] *A spade.* On the cover note the crossed spade and key above
the bundle.

[20] *Mrs. Sapsea's tomb.* It seems incredible to the writer that this
tomb had no important part to play after the trouble Jasper is made
to take to secure the key to it. At the same time one recoils from the
idea that Edwin is buried in a stranger's monument. Also the key
was returned the same night to Durdles' bundle, and there is no hint
given that an impression was taken of it or that it was borrowed on
Christmas Eve. We are led, therefore, to the conclusion that the important use made of the tomb was as a half-way-house for the imple-
ments required. The advantage was that had they been found there
by some mischance while the preparations were being made, there was
nothing to connect them with Jasper. In Drood's sarcophagus this
was not the case.

[21] *A Cavity.* As already stated this cavity is somewhat hypo-
thetical (*See Note in Episode I*). The cavity mentioned by Durdles
was not in Mrs. Sapsea's tomb. " Say Mrs. Sapsea. Her wall's
thicker, but say Mrs. Sapsea."

door. The spade stands in the corner. All is now
prepared. Jasper puts out the light and leaves the
place, locking the door behind him. The Sapsea outer
door he had already locked before entering the Drood
sarcophagus.

Still in the shadow, he takes the lantern back to
the Crypt, lets himself in by the same door that let him
out, finds Durdles still asleep and puts the crypt key
by his hand, ties the Sapsea key up in the bundle and
wakens Durdles by walking up and down noisily beating
his hands and stamping his feet. Durdles, his dream now
over, awakes to a perception of the lanes of light really
changed much as he had dreamed. He asks the time.

"Hark! the bells are going in the Tower."

"Two!" cries Durdles, scrambling up. "Why
did'nt you try to wake me Mr. Jasper?" "I did.
I might as well have tried to wake the dead." "Did
you touch me?" "Touch you! Yes, shook you."
As Durdles recalls that touching something in his
dream, he looks down on the pavement, and sees the
key of the crypt door lying close to where he himself lay.
"I dropped you, did I? he says, picking it up and re-
calling that part of his dream. He is again conscious
of being watched by his companion.[22] "Well," says
Jasper smiling "are you quite ready? Pray don't
hurry." "Let me get my bundle right, Mister Jarsper,
and I'm with you."

[22] *Watched by his Companion.* It is no longer Durdles' state of
intoxication that Jasper watches, but his state of comprehension.
How much has he noticed? Does he suspect anything? Durdles
reverses the position when he asks of what Jasper suspects him?

As he ties it afresh he is once more conscious that
he is very narrowly observed. "What do you suspect
me of Mister Jarsper," he asks ? " I've no suspicions
of you my good Mr. Durdles, but I have suspicions that
my bottle was filled with something stiffer than either
of us supposed. And I also have suspicions that its
empty." Durdles condescends to laugh at this. Con-
tinning to chuckle he rolls to the door and unlocks it.
They both pass out and Durdles relocks it and pockets
the key. " A thousand thanks for a curious and interesting night " says Jasper, " you can make your own
way home ? " Each is turning his own way when
Deputy appears.

"What ! is that baby devil on the watch [23] there ! "
cries Jasper and rushes at him, collars him and tries
to bring him across. " Don't hurt the boy, Mister
Jarsper," urges Durdles. " Recollect yourself." " He
followed us to-night when we first came here." " Yer
lie, I didn't," replies Deputy, in his only form of polite
contradiction. " He has been prowling near us ever
since ! " " Yer lie, I haven't " returns Deputy. " I'd
only just come out for my 'elth when I see you two a
coming out of the Kinfreederel." " Take him home,
then " retorts Jasper ferociously, though with a strong
check upon himself. They depart, Deputy stoning
Durdles home.

[23] *On the Watch.* Jasper in his fear and fury lets us see just what
he dreads. " He followed us when we first came here. He has been
prowling near us ever since. He has seen all I have done to-night."
His relief at Deputy's lie " I'd only just come out," is intense. Deputy
had really seen something but not much. Probably he had seen Jasper
enter the Crypt alone after 1 a.m. The manuscript note in " Plans,"
is " Keep the boy suspended."

Jasper goes to his Gatehouse brooding. And thus the unaccountable expedition comes to an end for the time being.

EPISODE IV.

THE ENGAGED COUPLE.

EPISODE IV.

THE ENGAGED COUPLE.

ROSA Bud, at the opening of the story, was a young and pretty little creature very like her mother had been. She was an orphan, both her parents having died before she was seven years old. Her mother was drowned at a party of pleasure on the river and her father died of grief on the first anniversary of that hard day. She had no other relative that she knew of in the world. Rosa's guardian, Mr. Grewgious, was not a relative, but had been her father's friend for many years.

Rosa was engaged to marry Edwin Drood as everyone in chattering Cloisterham knew. Their two fathers had been fast friends and old college companions and the betrothal of Rosa by anticipation to Drood's son grew out of Drood's soothing of Bud's year of mental distress.

When first they plighted their troth to one another, Rosa's father had given her mother a ring—a rose of diamonds and rubies delicately set in gold. This ring he took from her dead finger in Grewgious' presence and when his own death drew near he placed it in Grewgious' hands upon this trust—that Edwin and Rosa growing to manhood and womanhood and being betrothed and their betrothal prospering and coming to maturity, Grewgious should give the ring to Edwin to place upon Rosa's finger to seal their compact.

The marriage was fixed for the month of May in 1843, when Edwin would be of age. His father (now buried at Rochester) had been a partner in a firm of Engineers operating in Egypt, and on coming of age Edwin would attain an interest in the partnership. Until then he was a charge upon the firm, and his maternal uncle Jasper was his guardian and trustee.

This betrothal of the two friends' children to one another by their fathers, was a wish, a sentiment, a friendly project tenderly expressed upon both sides. It was nothing more. There was to be no forfeiture of property on either side if it did not lead to marriage. But the pair, when they were both children began to be accustomed to it, and grew up accustomed to it, and so had come to be, as they were when the story opens, an engaged couple.

But though resigned to their situation, Rosa and Edwin were not happy in it, each felt the irksomeness of not being free to choose in such a matter. Rosa found it absurd to be an engaged orphan and to have the girls and the servants scuttling about after her like mice in the wainscot when her affianced husband came to call on her—for even the young ladies at the Nun's house had it pat that a husband had been chosen for Rosa by will and bequest. And Edwin found it irritating to be so dictated to by dead and gone parents, and to have everyone in chattering old Cloisterham referring to it. " I wonder no public house has been set up with my portrait for the sign of ' the Betrothed's Head,' or ' Pussy's Portrait.' One or the other,'' he says in pique.

Yet Edwin would have drifted into their wedding day without a pause for real thought loosely trusting that all would go well left alone—would have done so but for Rosa and the ring.

The ring of diamonds and rubies held on trust to be the engagement ring of Edwin and Rosa was kept by Mr. Grewgious locked in an escritoire in his chambers in Staple Inn. His intention had been to take it down to Rochester with him on his promised visit to Rosa at Christmas, and then to give it to Edwin to place upon her finger. But Edwin happened to visit Grewgious in his chambers before journeying down to Rochester (where he was to make the final irrevocable preparations for his marriage), and on this visit to Mr. Grewgious he shewed such coolness, lassitude, doubt, indifference, disclosed a state of mind half smoke, half fire, and so unlike that Mr. Grewgious looked for in a true lover, that Grewgious decided to fulfil his trust by handing the ring to Edwin then and there in the presence of Bazzard, his clerk, as witness, and to make the solemnity the occasion of this appeal to Edwin : " Your placing it on her finger," giving him the ring, " will be the solemn seal upon your strict fidelity to the living and the dead. If anything should be amiss, if anything should be even slightly wrong between you, if you should have any secret consciousness that you are committing yourself to this step for no higher reason than because you have long been accustomed to look forward to it ; then I charge you once more by the living and the dead to bring that ring back to me."

That serious putting him on his trust to the living

and the dead, brought Edwin to a check. He must either give the ring to Rosa or he must take it back. " I will be guided by what she says and by how we get on " was his decision.

Rosa, meanwhile, on her side, had long been thinking about abandoning their intended relations and had at last summoned up the courage to make the suggestion.

" Eddy, let us be courageous. Let us change to brother and sister from this day forth." " Never be husband and wife ? " " Never ! you are not truly happy in our engagement. I am not truly happy in it. If we knew yesterday, and we did know yesterday and on many, many yesterdays that we were far from right together in these relations which were not of our own choosing, what better could we do to-day than change them ? "

Her full heart breaking into tears he puts his arm about her waist and they walk by the river side together. She tells of Grewgious' visit to her and he of his to Grewgious. The ring ! His right hand was in his breast seeking the ring ; but he checked it as he thought " If I am to take it back, why should I tell her of it ? Let them be, let them lie unspoken of in his breast."

Among the mighty store of wonderful chains that are for ever forging day and night in the vast ironworks of time and circumstance, there was one chain forged in the moment of that small conclusion [1] riveted to the

---

[1] *The Small Conclusion.* " All discovery of the murderer was to be baffled till towards the close when by means of a gold ring which had resisted the corrosive effects of the lime into which he had thrown the body, not only the person murdered was to be identified, but the locality of the crime, and the man who committed it." Forster, *Life of Charles Dickens.*

E

foundation of heaven and earth and gifted with invincible force to hold and drag.   They kissed each other fervently.

God bless you dear, goodbye !
God bless you dear, goodbye ! [2]

[2] *Goodbye.* Though they thought themselves to be parting as lovers only, this was really a final goodbye. Compare with it the passage in which Edwin takes leave of Rochester and the following extract from *Martin Chuzzlewit.* "It may be that the evening whispered to his conscience, or it may be (as it has been) that a shadowy veil was dropping round him closing out all thoughts but the presentiment and vague foreknowledge of impending doom. If there be fluids, as we know there are, which conscious of a coming wind or rain or frost, will shrink and strive to hide themselves in their glass arteries ; may not that subtle liquor of the blood perceive by properties within itself that hands are raised to waste and spill it ; and in the veins of men run cold and dull as his did in that hour ? "

EPISODE V.

THE GREEN-EYED MONSTER.

EPISODE V.

THE GREEN-EYED MONSTER.

(a) JASPER WARNS EDWIN.

"TAKE it as a warning then." In the act of having his hands released and of moving a step back Edwin pauses for an instant to consider the application of these last words. The instant over, he says "The disinterestedness of your painfully laying your inner self bare as a warning to me," Mr. Jasper's steadiness of face and figure becomes so marvellous that his breathing seems to have stopped, "I really was not prepared for, as I may say, your sacrificing yourself to me in that way." Mr. Jasper becomes a breathing man again, shrugs his shoulders, laughs "you won't be warned then?" "No, Jack." "You can't be warned then?" "No, Jack." Mr. Jasper dissolves his attitude and they both go out together.

What is it all about? What does it mean? Jasper has had an attack after his opium bout. He has reposed in Edwin the confidence that he takes opium for a pain —an agony and is troubled with some stray sort of ambition, aspiration, restlessness, dissatisfaction.

"No wretched monk who droned his life away in that gloomy place before me can have been more tired of it than I am. He could take for relief (and did take) to carving demons out of the stalls and seats and desks.

What shall I do ?   Must I take to carving them out of my heart ? "

Jasper bids Edwin remember his state of mind and heart, and take it as a warning.   In the act of moving a step back, Edwin pauses for an instant to consider the application to himself of these last words. Jasper watches him, holding his breath at the very thought that Edwin is beginning to realise how he is threatened. The instant over " Your sacrificing yourself to me," says Edwin, and Jasper knows he has failed to understand the warning.   Instantly Jasper becomes a breathing man again and shrugs his shoulders. He won't and can't be warned !

(b)   Rosa's Confidence to Helena.

" Who is Mr. Jasper ?   You do not love him ? " " Ugh."   " You know that he loves you ? "   " Don't tell me of it.   He terrifies me, he haunts my thoughts like a dreadful ghost. I feel as if he could pass in through the wall when he is spoken of.   He has made a slave of me with his looks.   He has forced me to understand him without his saying a word ; and he has forced me to keep silence without his uttering a threat.   When I play he never moves his eyes from my hands.   When I sing he never moves his eyes from my lips.   When he plays a passage he himself is in the sounds whispering that he pursues me as a lover and commanding me to keep his secret.   To-night when he watched my lips so closely as I was singing, besides feeling terrified I felt ashamed and passionately hurt.   It was as if he kissed me and I couldn't bear it, but cried out.   You must never breathe this to anyone. But you said to-night that you would not be afraid of him under any circumstances and that gives me—who am so much afraid of him—courage to tell only you. Hold me! Stay with me! I am too frightened to be left by myself."

(c) NEVILLE'S OUTBURST.

" I have never yet had the courage to say to you, Sir, what in full openness I ought to have said when you first talked with me on this subject. It is not easy to say, and I have been withheld by a fear of its seeming ridiculous, which is very strong upon me down to this last moment, and might, but for my sister, prevent my being quite open with you even now—I admire Miss Bud,[1] Sir, so very much, that I cannot bear her being treated with conceit or indifference; and even if I did not feel that I had an injury against young Drood on my own account, I should feel that I had an injury against him on hers. I say that I love her and despise and hate him!"

(d) JASPER MISLED.

Plunged into a state of hopeless angularity by the spectacle of Miss Twinkleton's curtsey,[2] suggestive of marvels happening to her respected legs, Mr. Grewgious got out of the presence how he could. As he held it incumbent upon him to call on Mr. Jasper before leaving

---

[1] *I Admire Miss Bud.* Manuscript " Plans " has " Neville admires Rosa. That comes out from himself."

[2] *Miss Twinkleton's Curtsey.* This passage is a combination ot the text and manuscript.

Rochester, he went to the Gatehouse, but Mr. Jasper's door being closed and presenting on a slip of paper the word " Cathedral," Mr. Grewgious forthwith repaired thither to find the choir coming out. Among the dirty linen [3] that was already being unbuttoned behind with all the expedition compatible with a feint of following the mace in procession round the corner was the robe of Mr. Jasper. He threw it to a boy who sadly wanted " getting up " by some laundress, and he and Mr. Grewgious walked out of the Cathedral talking as they went. " Nothing is the matter ? " Mr. Jasper began rather quickly. " You have not been sent for ? " " Not at all, not at all. I came down of my own accord. I have had it in my mind to come down this long time. But more off than on, I am ashamed to say." " Are you going to————? " " I have been to my pretty ward's and am now homeward bound again. I merely came to tell her seriously what a betrothal by deceased parents is—that it could not be considered binding against any such reason for its dissolution as a want of affection or want of disposition to carry it into effect." " Had you any special reason for telling her that ? " Mr. Grewgious shrugged his shoulders [4] as he answered somewhat sharply, " The special reason of resolving to do my duty, Sir. Simply that. I assure you that this implies not the least doubt of or disrespect to your

[3] *The Dirty Linen.* The passages " among the dirty linen " to " talking as they went," and " Have had it in my mind " to " When are you going to ! " and several minor alterations are here inserted from the manuscript.
[4] *Shrugged his Shoulders.* Manuscript.

nephew. Duty in the abstract must be done,[5] even if
it did, but it did not and it does not. I like your nephew
very much. I hope you are satisfied ? ”   “ Can I be
less than satisfied ? ”

“ I will wager,” said Jasper smiling—his lips were
still so white that he was conscious of it and bit and
moistened them while speaking. “ I will wager that
she hinted no wish to be released from Ned ? ”   “ And
you will win your wager if you do, at least I suppose we
should [6] allow some margin for little maidenly delicacies.
What do you think ? ”   “ There can be no doubt of it.”
“ I am glad you say so because she seems to have some
little delicate instinct that all preliminary arrangements
had best be made between Mr. Edwin Drood and herself,
don’t you see ?   She don’t want us, don’t you know ? ”
Jasper touched himself on the breast and said somewhat
indistinctly “ You mean me.” Mr. Grewgious touched
himself on the breast and said “ I mean us.” “ Therefore,” said Mr. Grewgious in a cosily arranging manner,[7]
“ let them have their little discussions and councils
together when Mr. Edwin Drood comes here at Christmas,
and then you and I will step in and put the final touches
to the business.” “ So you settled with her that you
would come back at that time ” observed Jasper.
“ Eh ? ” said the other expressionlessly innocent. But

---

[5] *Duty . . . must be done.* Manuscript. Jasper answers
question with question because he is really the opposite of satisfied,
but does not intend Mr. Grewgious to know it. He was hoping against
hope that the pair would break off their engagement, hence his white-
lipped anxiety. Grewgious’ disclosure was a dire disappointment
to him.

[6] *At least I suppose we should.* Manuscript.

[7] *In a cosily arranging manner.* Manuscript.

not without adding internally " This is a very quick watch-dog ! " " So you settled with her that you would come back at Christmas " repeated Jasper. " At Christmas ? Certainly. Oh dear, yes. I settled with her that I would come back at Christmas," replied Mr. Grewgious as if the question had previously lain between Lady Day, Midsummer Day, and Michaelmas. By this time, sometimes walking very slowly and sometimes standing still they had reached the Gatehouse. " Will you not walk up," said Jasper " and refresh ? " " Thank you, no. I have a horse and chaise here and have not too much time to get across and catch the new railroad over yonder." Jasper pressed his hand [8] and they parted. When they next met, on the evening of Tuesday, the 27th December [9] Edwin was dead.

(e) JASPER ENLIGHTENED.

Unkempt and disordered, bedaubed with mud that had dried upon him, and with much of his clothing torn to rags [10] Jasper had but just dropped into his easy chair when Mr. Grewgious stood before him. " This is strange news," said Mr. Grewgious, " strange and fearful news."

[8] *Eh ? . . Jasper pressed his hand.* The whole of this passage is from the manuscript. " The new railroad over yonder," is the " remote fragment of main line," which passengers from Rochester joined at Maidstone Road. A horse and chaise to Strood or Rochester stations would be absurd ! (*See Appendix II*).

[9] *Tuesday, 27th December.* On Xmas day (Sunday) Neville was arrested. With the earliest light of the next morning men were at work upon the river until the next day dawned. All that day again the search went on, setting his watches for that night again Jasper went home exhausted.

[10] *Clothing torn to Rags.* Thus effectually hiding any traces there might have been of the murder or the lime.

" I have a communication to make that will surprise
you. At least it has surprised me." Jasper with a
groaning sigh turned wearily in his chair. " Shall I
put it off till to-morrow ? " said Mr. Grewgious. " Mind
I warn you that I think it will surprise you ! " More
attention and concentration came into John Jasper's
eyes as they caught sight of Mr. Grewgious smoothing
his head again and again looking at the fire, but now with
a compressed and determined mouth. " What is it ? "
demanded Jasper becoming upright in his chair. " To
be sure," said Mr. Grewgious provokingly slowly and
internally as he kept his eyes on the fire. " I might ·
have known it sooner ; she gave me the opening.[11]
but I am such an exceedingly angular man, that it
never occurred to me ; I took it all for granted."
" What is it ? " demanded Jasper once more. " This
young couple, the lost youth and Miss Rosa, my ward,
though so long betrothed, and so long recognising their
betrothal, and so near being married," Mr. Grewgious
saw a staring white face, and two quivering white lips
in the easy chair, and saw two muddy hands gripping
its sides. But for the hands he might have thought
he had never seen the face. " This young couple came
gradually to the discovery (made on both sides pretty
equally I think), that they would be happier and better,
both in their present and their future lives, as affectionate
friends, or say rather as brother and sister, than as husband and wife." Mr. Grewgious saw a lead-coloured

---

[11] *She gave me the opening.* " Rosa shook her head with an almost
plaintive air of hesitation in want of help," &c.

face in the easy chair, and on its surface dreadful starting drops or bubbles as if of steel.

"This young couple formed at length the healthy resolution of interchanging their discoveries, openly, sensibly and tenderly. They met for that purpose. They agreed to dissolve their existing and their intended relations for ever and ever." Mr. Grewgious saw a ghastly figure rise open-mouthed from the easy chair and lift its outspread hands towards its head. "Your nephew, however, forbore to tell you the secret for a few days and left it to be discharged by me, when I should come down to speak to you, and he would be gone. I speak to you and he is gone." Mr. Grewgious saw the ghastly figure throw back its head, clutch its hair with its hands and turn with a writhing action from him. "I have said now all I have to say, except that this young couple parted firmly, though not without tears and sorrow on the evening when you last saw them together.[12] Mr. Grewgious heard a terrible shriek, and saw no ghastly figure sitting or standing; saw nothing but a heap of torn and miry clothes upon the floor [13].

(f) CRISPARKLE'S CONFIDENCE.

When John Jasper recovered from his fit or swoon he found himself being tended by Mr. and Mrs. Tope.

---

[12] *When you last saw them together.* "He saw us as we took leave of each other poor fellow ! he little thinks we have parted."

[13] *A heap of torn and miry clothes upon the floor.* "Mr. Grewgious took no pains to conceal his implacable dislike of Jasper, yet he never referred it however distantly to" any sort of suspicion that he had murdered Edwin. "But he was a reticent as well as an eccentric man ; and he made no mention of a certain evening when he warmed his hands at the Gatehouse fire and looked steadily down upon a certain heap of torn and miry clothes upon the floor."

His visitor, wooden of aspect, sat 'stiffly in a chair,
watching his recovery. "Do you know," said Jasper
after a hurried meal and when he had sat meditating
for a few minutes " do you know that I find some crumbs
of comfort in the communication with which you have
so much amazed me ? I begin to believe it possible
that he may have disappeared from among us of his own
accord and may yet be alive and well." [14] Mr. Crisparkle came in at the moment and Jasper repeated this
to him. "I pray to Heaven it may turn out so,"
exclaimed Mr. Crisparkle. "Mr. Grewgious ought to
be possessed of the whole case." Jasper went on
"He shall not through any suppression of mine be
informed of a part of it and kept in ignorance of another
part of. it, I wish him to be good enough to understand
that the communication he has made to me has hope-
fully influenced my mind in spite of its having been
before this mysterious occurrence took place, profoundly
impressed against young Landless."

This fairness troubled the Minor Canon much. He felt
that he was not as open in his own dealing. He charged
against himself reproachfully that he had suppressed
so far the two points of a second strong outbreak
of temper against Edwin Drood on the part of Neville
and of the passion of jealousy [15] having to his own certain
knowledge flamed up in Neville's breast against him.

---

[14] *May yet be Alive and Well.* Dickens in manuscript " Plans "
describes this as " Jasper's artful use of the communication on his
recovery." It would suit Jasper equally well whether it was commonly
supposed that Edwin had absconded or that he had been murdered
by Neville. In either case suspicion would be diverted from himself.
[15] See next page.

He had been balancing in his mind, much to its distress, whether his volunteering to tell these two fragments of truth at this time would not be tantamount to a piecing together of falsehood in the place of truth. However, here was a model before him. He hesitated no longer. Expressing his absolute confidence in the complete clearance of his pupil from the least taint of suspicion, sooner or later, he avowed that his confidence in that young gentleman had been formed in spite of his confidential knowledge that his temper was of the hottest and fiercest, and that it was directly incensed against Mr. Jasper's nephew by the circumstance of his romantically supposing himself to be enamoured of the same young lady. The sanguine reaction manifest in Mr. Jasper was proof even against this unlooked for declaration.[16] It turned him paler ; but he repeated that he would cling to the hope he had derived from Mr. Grewgious, and that if no trace of his dear boy were found, leading to the dreadful inference that he had been made away with, he would cherish unto the last

[15] *Neville's Jealousy.* See above. Crisparkle's present candour to Jasper is thus traduced by Jasper to Rosa six months later on. " It was hawked through the late enquiries by Mr. Crisparkle that Landless had confessed to him that he was a rival of my lost boy."

[16] *This Unlooked for Declaration.* Neville's love for Rosa was news to Jasper and news of dreadful import to each of them.

Jasper made it thenceforth the one object of his wasted life to purge upon the gallows the inexpiable offence of Neville in loving Rosa. The disclosure turned Jasper pale and instantly induced a second rapid change of plan. Jasper could no longer support the absconding theory. He must stand out for murder at the hands of Neville. Hence his " sanguine reaction " is straight-way watered down and made dependent on the non-finding of any trace of Edwin. Steps are then taken by Jasper to secure that such traces shall be found.

stretch of possibility the idea that he might have absconded of his own wild will.

Now it fell out that Mr. Crisparkle going away from this conference still very uneasy in his mind took a memorable night walk.[17] He walked to Cloisterham Weir. He often did so, and consequently there was nothing remarkable in his footsteps tending that way. But the preoccupation of his mind so hindered him from planning any walk, or taking heed of the objects he passed that his first consciousness of being near the Weir was derived from the sound of the falling water close at hand.

" How did I come here ? " was his first thought as he stopped.

" Why did I come here ? " was his second. Then he stood intently listening to the water. A familiar passage in his reading about airy tongues that syllable men's names [18] rose so unbidden to his ear that he put it from him with his hand as if it were tangible. It was starlight. The water came over the Weir with its usual sound on a cold starlight night, and little could be

---

17 *A Memorable Night Walk*. This walk I believe to have been imposed upon Crisparkle by Jasper by " telepathy," " hypnotism," or " mesmerism " as in those days it would be called no doubt. The alternative theory is perhaps as likely that Jasper relied on Crisparkle's known habit of bathing at Cloisterham Weir for ensuring the discovery of Edwin's watch and pin placed there by Jasper for the purpose of their being so discovered.   The watch, it will be remembered had been wound at 2-20 p.m. on Xmas Eve and had run down when found in the water, Neville was arrested before mid-day on Christmas Day.   Unless therefore the watch had an exceptionally short run, it could not have run down in his possession.   If Jasper had it, as no doubt he had, he cannot have placed it in the water on the same night as the murder.

18 See next page.

seen of it ; yet Mr. Crisparkle had a strange idea that
something unusual hung about the place ! He reasoned
with himself. What was it ? Where was it ? Put
it to the proof. Which sense did it address ? No
sense reported anything unusual there. Knowing very
well that the mystery with which his mind was occupied
might of itself give the place this haunted air, he strained
those hawk's eyes of his for the correction of his sight.
Nothing in the least unusual was remotely shadowed
forth. But he resolved he would come back early in the
morning. The Weir ran through his broken sleep all
night and he was back again at sunrise. His eyes were
attracted keenly to one spot. It struck him that at
that ˙spot—a corner of the Weir—something glistened
which did not move and come over with the glistening
water drops but remained stationary. He plunged
into the icy water and swam for the spot ; climbing
the timbers he took from them caught among their
interstices by its chain a gold watch, bearing engraved
upon its back E.D.[19] He dived and dived and dived
until he could bear the cold no more. His notion was
that he would find the body ; he only found a shirt-
pin sticking in some mud and ooze.

[18] *Airy tongues that syllable Men's Names.*

MILTON —" COMUS."

" What might this be ? A thousand fantasies
   Begin to throng into my memory.
   Of calling shapes, and beck'ning shadows dire,
   And airy tongues that syllable men's names
   On sands and shores and desert wildernesses."

[19] *E.D.*—If (as some suppose) the murder was hallucination how
came this watch and pin to be where they were found ?

EPISODE VI.
MR. JASPER PROPOSES.

EPISODE VI.

MR. JASPER PROPOSES.

MR. JASPER is a dark man of some six and
twenty with thick lustrous well arranged black
hair, and whiskers. He looks older than he is
as dark men often do. His voice is deep and good, his
face and figure are good but his manner is a little sombre.

Lay Precentor, or Lay Clerk at Rochester Cathedral,
he has the reputation of having done wonders with the
choir there. He has the gift of teaching, and besides
training the choir also acts as music master to the girls
at the Nun's House School. Altogether he seems cut
out for his vocation. But he hates it ! Unknown to
others and unsuspected by Edwin even, he hates it
all. Jasper has long been secretly and desperately in
love with Rosa. Rosa, as we have seen, is bound
to Edwin and daily drawing nearer marriage. Jasper
has never spoken to Rosa about love. Never ! but he
has made a slave of her with his looks. He has forced
her to understand him without his saying a word.

Jasper is an opium smoker. He took to opium when
he could no longer bear his life ; his love and jealousy
in the cramping monotony of his existence became a
physical pain—an agony—which overcame him. He
took to opium to get relief. He got it. He got it at a
price. Carrying Rosa's image in his arms he wandered
through paradises in visions ; carrying her image in

his arms he rushed in visions through Hells. From Paradise and Hell alike he woke to the distasteful work of the day, and to the wakeful misery of the night.

Watching day by day the ill-matched pair—his nephew and his loved one—Jasper cherished to the last stretch of possibility the hope of their releasing one another and leaving his loved one to him. If not— and day by day the wretch's hope grew less as the arrangements for the marriage still went forward— if not Edwin must die. Jasper is resolved to kill him, and has his plans prepared. Finally he sees, or thinks he sees, the couple seal their parents' compact with a lover's kiss. That kiss has sealed the doom of Edwin who dies on Christmas Eve, strangled by Jasper secretly.

Six months and more elapse after the murder before Jasper ventures to renew pursuit of Rosa. Then, calling at the school and finding Rosa there alone, he forces her to come to him. Rosa chooses the open air, but even there he magnetises her. He stands leaning lightly on the sundial in the garden. She cannot resist his horrible complusion but sits down with bent head on the garden seat beside him. Both are in mourning. Jasper questions Rosa about her music lessons and her refusal to go on with them. She is angered and declines to be cross-questioned or to answer. His gloating admiration of the touch of anger on her, and of the fire and animation brought by it causes her rising spirit to fall again and she struggles with a sense of shame, affront and fear much as at his following of her lips when he was her music master. When she rises to go he makes her sit again by threatening her with harm to others if she does go. When he calls her " Dearest," " charming," " my beloved," she again starts up to go but his face is so wicked and menacing that her flight is arrested by horror as she looks at him. Frozen with fear she cannot flee him.

So arrested, so compelled, Rosa listens to her first proposal. Jasper declares to her his mad unholy love.

" Rosa, even when my dear boy was affianced to you I loved you madly, even when I strove to make him more ardently devoted to you, I loved you madly, even when he gave me the picture of your lovely face so carelessly traduced by him, which I feigned to hang always in my sight for his sake, but worshipped in torment for years, I loved you madly ; I endured it all in silence. So long as you were his or so long as I supposed you to be his, I hid my secret loyally did I not ? " Jasper's lie so gross, while the mere words in which it is told are so true is more than Rosa can endure. She answers with kindling indignation, " you were as false throughout, sir, as you are now, you were false to him daily and hourly. You know that you made my life unhappy by your pursuit of me. You know that you made me afraid to open his generous eyes and that you forced me for his own trusting good, good sake to keep the truth from him that you were a bad, bad man."

His preservation of his easy attitude rendering his working features and his convulsive hands absolutely diabolical, he returns with a fierce extreme of admiration. " How beautiful you are ! You are more beautiful in anger than in repose. I don't ask you for your love, give me yourself and your hatred ; give me yourself and that enchanting scorn ; it will be enough for me."

Impatient tears rise to the eyes of the trembling little beauty and her face flames. She rises to leave him in indignation. He detains her with a threat. " You care for your bosom friend's good name ; you care for her peace of mind, then remove the shadow of the gallows from her dear one ! "

" You dare propose to me to . . . "

" Darling I dare propose to you. Stop there. If it be bad to idolize you I am the worst of men ; if it be good I am the best. My love for you is above all other love. My truth to you is above all other truth. Let me have hope and favour and I am a forsworn man for your sweet sake. So that you take me were it even mortally hating me. I love you, love you, love you. If you were to cast me off now—but you will not ! You would never be rid of me ; no one should come between us. I would pursue you to the death ! "

The handmaid coming out to open the gate for him, he quietly pulls off his hat as a parting salute and goes away with no greater show of agitation than is visible in the effigy of Mr. Sapsea's father opposite. Rosa faints in going upstairs.

EPISODE VII.

ON SECRET SERVICE.

EPISODE VII.

ON SECRET SERVICE.

A T about this time—on Wednesday, July 5th to be precise—a stranger appeared in Rochester, Dick Datchery was the name he went by in that picturesque old city, Tartar was his name in London. Yesterday he was up the river with Rosa, Grewgious and Lobley in a row-boat. To-day he has come down the Thames in his yacht with Lobley from Greenhithe to Gravesend. Thence he has travelled on alone by road to Rochester where he now announces his intention of taking a lodging for a month or two with a view of settling down there altogether. Meanwhile, Rosa pines in Bloomsbury waiting for something that will not come, that never comes ! " Until as the days crept on and nothing happened the neighbours began to say that the pretty girl at Billickin's who looked so wistfully and so much out of the windows of the drawing room seemed to be losing her spirits."[1] Why this base desertion ? What had happened ?

To understand the situation, we must retrace our steps as far as the Midsummer Recess at the Nun's House. Not so far in time as in occurrences. That was last

---

[1] *Losing Her Spirits.* Let any reader who still doubts that it was for Tartar that Rosa was waiting and pining at Billickin's consider this passage :—

" The pretty girl might have lost her spirits but for the accident of lighting on some books of voyages and sea adventures. As a compensation against their romance Miss Twinkleton made the most of all the . . . . statistics; while Rosa listening intently made the most of what was nearest to her heart. So they both did better than before."

Monday, and to-day is only Wednesday. Then the High Street was musical with the cry in various silvery voices, "Goodbye, Rosebud darling!" and among the departing coaches carrying the young ladies to their several homes was one which carried Helena to attend her brother's fortunes in Staple Inn. Rosa remains and the same afternoon finds her alone, Mrs. Tisher being absent on leave and Miss Twinkletön having contributed herself and a veal pie to a picnic. Jasper calls, declares his mad love and announces his threat to Helena's peace of mind and to the life of Neville. Rosa the same night, flees to Grewgious and tells him all. Grewgious hears her story understandingly and begs to be told a second time those parts which bear on Helena and Neville. Next day, Tuesday, Tartar and Rosa meet and fall in love. "Poor, poor Neville!" Helena divines the facts and seems to compassionate somebody. "My poor Neville." But Rosa's tale of Jasper's threatenings requires attention. "Would it be best," Helena wonders "to wait until any more maligning and pursuing of Neville on the part of this wretch shall disclose itself or to try and anticipate it so far as to find out whether any such goes on darkly about them in Staple Inn? Neville has not so much as exchanged a word with anyone but Mr. Tartar there. Now if Mr. Tartar would call to see him openly and often; if he would spare a minute for the purpose frequently; if he would even do so almost daily; something might come of it.[2]"

---

[2] "*Something might come of it.*" No wonder Rosa is perplexed. Helena's plan was nearly as nebulous as that "something" which Mr. Micawber was expecting to turn up.

"Something might come of it, dear?" repeated Rosa with a highly perplexed face. "Something might?"

"If Neville's movements are really watched and if the purpose really is to isolate him from all friends and acquaintances and wear his daily life out grain by grain (which would seem to be the threat[3] to you) does it not appear likely[4] that his enemy would in some way communicate with Mr. Tartar to warn him off from Neville?"

"I see," cries Rosa, and Mr. Tartar at once declares his readiness to act and to enter on his task that very day. What then is Mr. Tartar doing at Rochester the very next day. What of his promise? What of Helena's hope to hear of Rosebud from Mr. Tartar? No wonder Rosa is like to lose her spirits looking and waiting in vain for the sailor to call at Billickin's.

But we have forgotten Grewgious. He was no party to Helena's suggested plan[5] of action. He was no party to Helena's misunderstanding of what was threatened. He had Rosa's narration clearly put away and knew that "the gallows" was the threat to Neville not "isolation." The peace of mind to be disturbed was Helena's not Neville's. Mr. Grewgious held

---

[3] "*Which would seem to be the threat.*" Helena had not understood. Perhaps Rosa had toned down to her the threat of "the shadow of the gallows," for her dear one. Mr. Grewgious on the other hand, perfectly understood what Jasper threatened.

[4] "*Does it not appear likely.*" Yes, if the hypothesis be granted; but if the hypothesis was mistaken the inference loses its foundation.

[5] *Grewgious no party to Helena's plan.* He was specially consulted about the desirability of taking action and agreed, but was markedly *not* consulted about the particular action suggested.

decidedly to the general principle that if you could steal a march upon a brigand or a wild beast you had better do it ; and he also held decidedly to the special case that John Jasper was a brigand and a wild beast in combination. But he never endorsed Helena's plan. He had a plan of his own as he had told them. Jasper hoped by watching Neville in Staple Inn so to accumulate circumstances against him, so to direct, sharpen and point them that they might slay him. Why not turn his weapon against himself and thus steal a march upon him ? By perseverance the missing link, the wanting clue which would prove his guilt might be discovered and the shadow of the gallows be shifted to him and the burden of unjust suspicion be removed for ever from young Landless. Why not set a watch on Jasper at Rochester, the counterpart of the watch he keeps on Neville here in Staple ? If so, what better watchman than this young sailor, Tartar, so keen on Rosa and unknown or scarcely known to Jasper ? But will he undertake the task ? Mr. Grewgious will put it to him.

Rosa is safely tucked in bed at Furnivals and dreaming of the everlastingly green garden and the beanstalk country and the Admiral's cabin—and perhaps the Admiral. The lieutenant, meanwhile, is seated in Grewgious' chair in Grewgious' chambers being fully confided in by Mr. Grewgious.

Mr. Crisparkle, able now to reassure the anxious Miss Twinkleton and to arrange for her to join Rosa at Billickins' on Thursday, has returned to Rochester. His short summary to Tartar of the distresses of Neville and his sister has paved the way for the fuller and more

particular account of the whole mysterious story which
Grewgious is now in course of giving Tartar. Bazzard
is not about.[6] It is night time and long past office hours.
Tartar has been told already of Edwin's relations to
Rosa and to Jasper and of his mysterious disappearance
last Christmas. He now learns from Grewgious of
Jasper's pursuit of Rosa as a lover. Anger springs up
in Tartar. " Yesterday," continues Grewgious, " the
scoundrel dared openly to propose to her," and he joins
to this a lucid and precise account to Tartar of the
exact terms in which Jasper had dared to threaten and
propose to Rosa. " Damn him, how dare he ! " No
question now if Tartar will help unmask him ! The
villain ! To force his horrid shameless love on that
young, innocent, unprotected lady ! Damn him again !
And now to plans for her protection and the disclosure
of his villainy. The man takes opium. So much
Grewgious knows from Rosa who got it from Edwin.
Tick that off. He had ample motive for murder in his
raging jealousy fed by the parting kiss he saw and mis-
interpreted. Tick that off. Jealousy of a new rival—
Neville—has urged him on to six months' silent labour
in the effort to bring the latter to the gallows and burning
jealousy still spurs him on. But we may doubt if pru-
dent Mr. Grewgious told this to Tartar just yet. Sufficient for Lieutenant Tartar that Jasper is bent on
fabricating evidence which shall bring Neville to trial
and conviction. He must be watched and his plan

6 *Bazzard is not about.* He is " off duty there altogether just at
present " it will be remembered.

prevented. Will Lieutenant Tartar undertake the task?
His yacht down Greenhithe way might be taken round
to Gravesend and Lieutenant Tartar might appear at
Rochester a stranger. Some slight disguise—a wig for
instance—would be advisable on the off chance of Jasper
having noticed him in Staple.

Tartar hesitates an instant. The plan will mean
indeterminate exile from Miss Rosa! He can hardly
bring that reason before her guardian just at present,
however. After all, he only met his love this morning
as time goes on this planet! His promise to visit Neville
daily is urged in explanation of his slowness to respond,
by which, as he sees, Grewgious is puzzled and disappointed. But for that, he tells him, he would jump
at any sort of opportunity to serve Miss Rosa and the
others. Grewgious is relieved. " If that is all," he
will undertake to obtain absolution from the promise
and plausibly to explain Tartar's absence to the Landlesses—" Miss Rosa too? " suggests the sailor. " I
think it wisest that she shall know nothing of this as
yet," says Mr. Grewgious, " but if she asks after you,
as no doubt she will, I will explain to her that you are
absent on her service." With that poor consolation
Tartar must be content.

So now we know how it comes about that Rosa
pines and peaks in gritty London, and Tartar in his wig
and pseudonym of Datchery takes lodgings at the Topes,
in Rochester and lounges about the Precincts like the
chartered bore of the city.

In a detective the bold step is the wise one. He
confronts Jasper in his own room face to face at once,

and so he gets to know and be known by him.   He also
gets to know the Mayor and to be well established with
him.   As a cat watches a mouse hole so he takes his
post with open door and watches Jasper's postern
entrance opposite.   He misses no opportunity of getting
to know the lowly local characters.   Deputy and he
are "Winks" and "Dick," and Durdles is open to
seeing him any evening if he brings liquor for two with
him.   So things are going famously when another
stranger appears in Rochester.   She turns in under the
archway just after Jasper has arrived there and gone
up his postern staircase.   Tartar seeing her brought to
a standstill asks whom she is looking for ?   "A gentleman in mourning [7] who passed in there this minute," is
her answer.   So she wants Jasper does she ?   What
can her business be with him ?   Told his dwelling and his
name she does not go to see him, but asks his calling.
She seems to want to see and hear him singing in the
choir.   Odd that !   Where does she come from ?
Jasper and the others have just come back from town.
Is she from London too ?   She does not answer that.
Is she after money ?   Tartar rattles the loose money in
his trouser pockets.   Yes, she asks for money to pay
for her traveller's lodging—where Winks is servant.
She knows that place then.   Has she been here often ?
Once in all her life she says.   What's that ?   Opium !
The plot begins to thicken.   She seeks Jasper who takes
opium and she takes opium.   More to follow.   The
last time she was here was Christmas Eve when a young

[7] *In Mourning.*   Manuscript.

gentleman gave her three and sixpence and the young
gentleman's name was Edwin and she asked him if he
had a sweetheart and he said he hadn't. Phew! That
must have been Edwin Drood after he had jilted Rosa! [8]
Tartar could get no more from her just then without
asking dangerous questions so gives her the three and
six she asked him for and lets her go her way. Little
enough he has learned, and yet there is promise in it.
Probably, however, she merely wants to sell Jasper
more opium. But why see him at 7 o'clock in the
Cathedral if that is all? Anyhow Tartar will see if she
really does go there and meantime he will get Winks
to find out where she comes from—exactly where she
lives. The knowledge may prove useful. John Jasper's
lamp is kindled, and his lighthouse is shining when
Tartar returns, alone, towards it. As mariners on a
dangerous voyage approaching an iron-bound coast
may look along the beams of the warning light to the
haven lying beyond it that may never be reached so the
sailor-detective's wistful gaze is directed to this beacon
and beyond. Having fetched his hat Tartar goes out
again and discovers Deputy or rather " Winks." Good!
Winks confirms that she is an opium smoker from London and is going to the " Kin-free-der-el," as Winks
pronounces it, in the morning. " We are getting on!"
Still a moderate stroke Tartar concludes, is all that he
is justified in scoring up as yet.

Next morning, in the Cathedral, the service is pretty

---

[8] *After he had jilted Rosa.* This is scarcely fair to Edwin but we
must bear in mind that Tartar never knew him and was himself in
love with Edwin's rejected fiancée.

well advanced, before Tartar can discern the opium woman. She is behind a pillar carefully withdrawn from Jasper's view, but regards him with the closest attention. All unconscious of her presence he chants and sings. She grins when he is most musically fervid and—yes, Tartar sees her do it !—shakes her fist at him behind the pillar's friendly shelter. Tartar looks again to convince himself. Yes again ! She hugs herself in her lean arms and then shakes both fists at the leader of the choir.

The service over Tartar accosts her outside the Cathedral. " Well, Mistress, Good-morning. You have seen him ? " " I've seen him deary ; I've seen him ! Know him ! Better far than all the Reverend Parsons put together know him.'

Before sitting down to his neat, clean breakfast, Tartar opens his corner cupboard door ; takes his bit of chalk from its shelf ; adds one thick line to the score extending from the top of the cupboard door to the bottom ; and then falls to with an appetite. No wonder ! Patience and perseverance are bringing their reward. This woman knows Jasper for what he is. She hates him. He does not know it. She lives in London and has followed him down here. Jasper will return to her. That will give the sought for opportunity against him. With the woman as an ally, Tartar may be spectator of his opium ravings and learn his secrets from him. Good indeed !

EPISODE VIII.

LANDLESS PROPOSES.

G

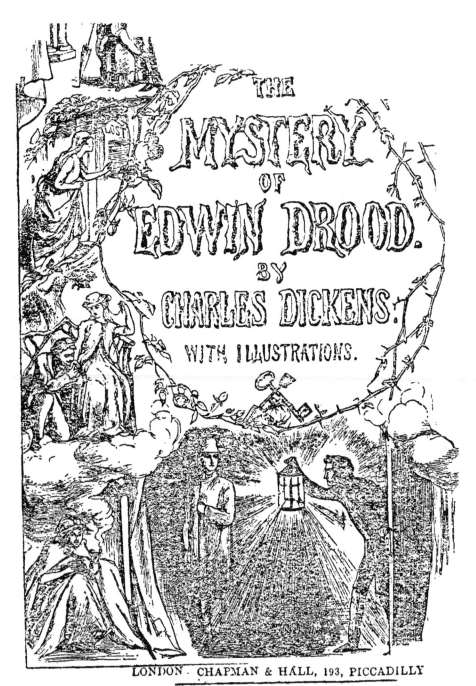

THE MYSTERY OF EDWIN DROOD.

BY CHARLES DICKENS.

WITH ILLUSTRATIONS.

LONDON. CHAPMAN & HALL, 193, PICCADILLY

Advertisements to be sent to the Publishers, and ADAMS & FRANCIS, 59, Fleet

EPISODE VIII.

LANDLESS PROPOSES.[1]

WHILST Tartar was away at Rochester [2] the days dragged very heavily with Rosa. The gritty state of things had few reliefs. London waited and waited always for someone who never came.

To Neville, too, in Staple Inn, the days were often long and listless. Whilst he has Helena with him things are better but her school holidays are drawing to a close, and she has to return to Rochester to-morrow. Neville will then be solitary once again. The promise made to

---

[1] *Landless Proposes.* The details of this scene are necessarily pure hypothesis, but the evidence for the scene itself is on the cover. It has been suggested that the kneeling figure kissing Rosa's hand is Jasper or else Tartar. But each of these is shewn elsewhere upon the cover and neither is the kneeling figure. The only certain clue to the identity of the latter is his moustache. Which character, if any, had a moustache? The answer seems at first to be that no moustache is mentioned. But the school-girls at the Nuns' house knew better. "Nothing escapes their notice, sir." Recall the quarrel scene acted by Neville and Edwin and imitated by the Misses Ferdinand and Giggles. "Neville flings the dregs of his wine at Edwin Drood, and is in the act of flinging the goblet after it, when his arm is caught in the nick of time by Jasper." "Miss Ferdinand got into new trouble by surreptitiously clapping on a paper moustache at dinner-time and going through the motions of aiming a water-bottle at Miss Giggles who drew a table-spoon in self defence." On Miss Ferdinand's evidence we shall be safe in saying that Neville wore moustaches. Clearly then it is he who kneels at Rosa's feet kissing her hand upon the cover. The rustic seat gives the clue to where the scene took place. Even now the garden of Staple Inn would make a pretty setting for a love scene. In 1842, it was neither so public as now it is nor yet so small. (*See Appendix II*).

[2] *Tartar away at Rochester.* As Datchery (*See Episode VII*).

visit him by Mr. Tartar has not been kept. Mr. Crisparkle's visits are as frequent as he can make them,
but he lives in distant Rochester, and cannot often get
to town. Mr. Grewgious is not far off, but he is a busy
man and no great company. Left to himself, Neville's
disposition is to work too hard and long, stay in all day
and walk only at night. Meanwhile, day and night,
he cannot cease to dream of Rosa or put her image from
his. mind. While young Drood was alive he pledged
himself to do so and achieved a measure of success.
Now he cannot cease to think of her. At last, the Minor
Canon being in London for a couple of nights, Neville
plucks up enough courage to beg for release from the
pledge he gave not to make known to Rosa his love for
her. He has kept his compact faithfully. Its cause
has gone now. Surely he may be released ? Reluc-
tantly, since it cannot be withheld, consent is given.
But, for his own sake, his sister and the Minor Canon view
the growth of his resolve to tell his love with gravest
apprehension. Helena knows that Rosa's heart is
given elsewhere, and fears the shock to Neville. Added
to which is the fear of Jasper's jealous rage should
Neville's proposal to Rosa reach his ears. To gain a
little respite Helena makes the suggestion that she and
the Minor Canon—if he can spare the time—shall call
on Rosa in Bloomsbury Square this afternoon. It
would be well to sound Rosa first, and ascertain that
she would not be likely to take ill, as yet, Neville's
proposal, seeing how short a time, comparatively, has
passed since Eddy's death—assuming indeed that he is
dead. To which Helena adds that she herself wants to

see Miss Twinkleton to learn the arrangements made for their journey down to Rochester to-morrow. Neville yields and so the matter remains for the present undecided. Crisparkle gladly escorts Helena to Bloomsbury and Neville remains alone. While they are away Rosa suddenly appears to Neville's view [3] to his amazement and delight, entering the pretty garden down below his window. In Bloomsbury Square there was little of comfort or delight on that hot afternoon in early autumn. Packing and plans and bickerings between Miss Twinkleton and the ever victorious, ever lugubrious Billickin. Uncertainty and dust and grittiness on all sides. Rosa will get away from it and spend the afternoon at Staple Inn she thinks. Now that Miss Twinkleton is leaving, new plans are to be made for Rosa. What more natural than that she should call on her guardian to learn them from him? What can the visit have to do with Mr. Tartar? He is not now at Staple. Does not Rosa know he left there a good while back? Yes, he keeps his chambers on, the porter thinks. No, he can't say where he is. No, nor when he will return. So Rosa visits P.J.T. [4] to find that her guardian is not in at present. Bazzard is there but he is not communicative and does not invite Rosa to step inside. Rosa tells him she will await Mr. Grewgious' return, outside in the garden.

[3] *Rosa appears to Neville's View.* A visit to Staple Inn will satisfy the reader that this would be so. Neville's, Tartar's and Grewgious' rooms are all carefully identified by Dickens.

[4] *Rosa Visits P.J.T.* P.J.T. means " John Thompson Principal 1797," but it needs "no matter-of-fact identification here." For present purposes let it mean " Perhaps John Thomas or Perhaps Joe Tyler," who Possibly Jabbered Thus.

Thus, simply, it comes about that Neville looking aimlessly out of his window sees Rosa tripping down the steps of Grewgious' chambers and visiting the lovely little garden of the Inn, where the dust-laden air is cooled by the small stream of the spouting fountain on this hot afternoon which bees are rendering drowsy.

Neville will go down to her. She sits beneath a tree upon a rustic seat with room for two. There Neville joins her. She tells him of the reason of her visit. It is to see her guardian. He is out at present. She must await his return to learn his plans for her, as she expects to have to leave London to-morrow or some day soon she knows not when. To go? She knows not whither nor cares a great deal. No! certainly not to Rochester! She shudders at the thought. Never there again! Neville attributes Rosa's agitation to the Mystery which has blighted both their lives. He has heard nothing [5] of the scene in that other garden with Jasper in it. They have kept it from him. He merely knows that Jasper has spoken to Rosa about himself, and has disclosed to her that his hatred of him endures as though he still believed him guilty of the murder. Neville has no thought of Jasper as a jealous rival. He does not guess how Rosa fears the man and shudders at her recollection of him.

---

[5] *He has heard nothing of Jasper's Proposal.* The whole story had been told to Helena it is true, but " I suppose " pursued Helena doubtfully " that he must know by and by all you have told me ; but I am not sure. Ask Mr. Crisparkle's advice my darling. Ask him whether I may tell Neville as much or as little of what you have told me as I think best." The Minor Canon was for the free exercise of Helena's judgment.

· By way of preface to what he is come down to say to her, Neville alludes sadly to the tribulations through which they have passed—and yet must pass—together. With mournful air he begs her forgiveness for his share in having caused her sorrow, especially for his foolish quarrel with Edwin. She would stop him if she could but what can she do or say ? She cannot make excuses and go ; for Neville has just heard from her own lips that she awaits her guardian there—if only he would come ! She cannot refuse to hear Neville, or surely he will suppose himself not merely not forgiven, but even not unsuspected of Eddy's death. Embarrassed and apprehensive of what next he is about to say—for she cannot but suspect to what all this is tending—she listens to the impulsive outburst of his pleading, looking away from him and nervously toying with a streamer from her summer hat.

She answers confusedly that he would have her pardon if it were a case for pardoning and adds that she never has suspected him of anything but honest and open dealing with poor, poor Eddy. Neville at these words lets his hat which he has been holding in his hand fall upon the ground [6] and going on one knee, seizes Rosa's nearest idle hand and covers it with kisses. His passionate nature can no longer bear restraint, and his long pent feelings declare themselves in a, torrent of ardent tones and words. His love is more than half declared, when Rosa snatches back her hand, starts from the seat, and in a low and strangled voice cries look !

[6] *Hat upon the ground.* The details of this scene are taken from the cover.

look ! Neville looks and sees the sailor Tartar
approaching [7] He has just turned in under the archway
closely followed by Mr. Grewgious. Did he see them ?
What must he think ? What shall she say or do ?
These thronging questions are driving Rosa half-dis-
tracted.   Tartar, a little distant in his manner perhaps,
greets Rosa with a cool " good afternoon, Miss Bud,"
raising his hat. To Neville, Tartar merely says " I
notice Mr. Landless that your interest in flowers is not
diminished." Mr. Grewgious who, with his short sight,
evidently has noticed nothing, invites the whole party to
step up to his chambers. But .Tartar, raising his hat
again, begs pardon if he has already intruded too much
on Miss Bud's time and private business or inconvenienced
her by keeping her guardian away overlong.   While
Neville on his part mutters some excuse in a strangled

---

[7] *Tartar approaching . . Jasper was standing there.* Jasper has
come to town pursuing Neville and Datchery pursuing Jasper.
   Learning from Mrs. Tope that Jasper is going " to get some
medicine," in town, Datchery divines that Jasper will visit the opium
woman during the night and lays his plans accordingly. First he
visits her himself and arranges to be let in by her after Jasper is asleep
—but before he begins to talk if possible. Datchery will come from the
docks disguised as a common sailor. This settled, Datchery returns
to his yacht and resumes his own personality as Tartar. Then he goes
to Furnival's for lunch, and there meets Grewgious, and is returning
with him to his chambers to report progress when turning in under the
inner arch of Staple, he sees Neville on his knees to Rosa. Meanwhile
Jasper has been to his hotel in Aldersgate and then either by chance
or by arrangement has come in contact with the clerk Bazzard in Staple
Inn, from whom he has learnt the story of the ring. Jasper is still
hanging around Staple when Rosa arrives and he sees Neville hastening
down to greet her. From the landing window he watches the whole
scene which adds fresh fuel to his rage against Neville and decides him
to instant action. He will get the ring at once, on his return, and
cause it to be found in Neville's Chambers. That will hang him if
any evidence *can* hang a man thinks Jasper.

tone and hurries off without his hat until called back to be handed it by Mr. Tartar with a sweeping bow. Mr. Grewgious seems a little puzzled by the turn events have taken, but asks Tartar if it would inconvenience him too much to look in later—say ten o'clock to-morrow morning? Mr. Crisparkle will, he hopes, be there. This Tartar promises that he will do and takes his leave. Rosa, red and white and much perturbed wishes a hurried good-bye to him and Neville and precedes her guardian up the steps into his chambers. Rosa's agitation would have been much increased had she been aware of yet another spectator of Neville's action. This spectator might have been seen from Mr. Grewgious' first floor window to take the form of a slinking individual, standing at the second floor landing window of the second house from the left corner of the Inn. It was Jasper standing there [7] watching the proposal of his deadly-hated rival to his beloved. All but fainting with fury, his countenance convulsed and purple, clenched teeth and staring eyes, Jasper stands glowering in the shadow and with his empty hands claws first the empty air then seems to throttle someone. An evil action! He laughs aloud when Tartar comes upon the scene and breaks it up. First watching them part, Jasper then slinks away himself and leaves the Inn.

EPISODE IX.

THE THIRD DAWN.

EPISODE IX.

THE THIRD DAWN.

THE scene of this episode is familiar to you. In that meanest and closest of small rooms Eastward and still Eastward of Aldersgate it is dark as yet. The favourite customer is there already, and lies dressed and drugged across the large unseemly broken-down bed groaning beneath the weight it bears. Listen! He begins to mutter! The tattered hag sets her face to his to catch his mumblings. Jasper takes no heed of her. A third figure lies across the bed—a maudlin sailor. He also sprawls and shifts about and draws up close to the talking dreamer throwing a tattooed arm about his neck. Removing the arm violently from him, Jasper rises bolt upright into a sitting posture. " Loose me " he shrieks. Then adds more calmly. " The noose is not for me but him, see! Landless! there! " and points. Falling back on to one elbow he goes on talking in a low but forceful tone. " At last the reaping. He is mine—my lawful prey. He will not break this net. He cannot. The bird will not escape *this* fowler. The snare is set too well. He's mine. The clue is found. The clue is found. The link. The ring. It must still be there. I will go get it. Now! To-night. It did not come back. Bazzard is certain. Father and son together." The sodden sailor has lain quiet all this while, heedless of his arm caught under the body of Jasper when he fell back on it. Now, at the name of **Bazzard**, he stirs a little and moves his arm. The action seems to waken Jasper from his dream and stupor. The focus of his eyes is changed from far to near. He sees the room, he sees the bed, he sees the sailor. Furiously he turns upon the hostess and assails her in language suited to the sordid den. Translated, he asks her what she means by letting unmentionable people come there and spy upon him? He grasps the sailor by the arm and asks him who the blank he is and what the blank he wants there? The woman shrinks and trembles and calls him dearie and offers him another pipe of comfort and whines she can't afford to shut out custom with trade so slack and the market price so dreffle high just now.

But the sailor is in a different humour, and slings his tattooed arm round Jasper's neck again and hugs and kisses him! Half smothers him! Not less furious now, but oddly relieved, Jasper shakes off the sailor, brushes aside the woman and the pipe she offers him, and struggling to the window looks out upon the breaking dawn. The woman watches him with furtive glances. The sailor sings a sea-ditty of dubious meaning with voice and breath that speak of gin as much as opium. Clinging to the crazy curtains Jasper has much ado to collect his scattered normal consciousness. Having come to himself earlier than is his wont, he has not enjoyed the sequence of Kaleidoscopic colours and the Eastern Pageant. By a mighty effort and with many a shudder he succeeds at last in shaking off the drowsiness upon him and is more or less himself. Still furious with the woman he flings her money roughly, reaches down his hat and stamps out through the door and down the creaking stairs with no good-morrow given to the rat-ridden door-keeper beneath them. Though he frequently looks back, as if expecting it, he is not followed as he makes his way, on foot first, to his cheap hotel in Aldersgate, and then by train to Rochester.

Meanwhile, as soon as the stairs have ceased to creak to Jasper's tread, the sailor quits the bed and asks the hag for water. When she has shambled off to get him some the sailor slips off an upper pair of seaman's trousers worn over the pantaloons of a man of means if not of fashion. The woman returning with a cracked jug with water in it he pours some in the basin and with the assistance of a piece of yellow soap and vigorous rubbing transforms his stained and made up face and grubby neck and hands to those of clean and sunburnt Tartar. Next he rinses out his mouth and gargles to wash away the taste of vilest gin. The woman whines to him it was as potent as she dared to make it to get him to talk at all. Who'd ha thought he'd wake like that before he'd scarce begun to tell them anything ? She calls Tartar " Sir," and whines she'll do better with the devil next time when she gets him all along o' her lone self. She'll make him talk then ! She'll make him talk dearie—sir, she means. Bless you sir, when he first came here he'd lay like that for hours, and then when it was later, he'd begin to sing and 'd keep on singing right through the night.

Tartar seems too much occupied in getting the look and smell and taste and atmosphere of the place out of his eyes and nose and mouth and mind, to pay much heed to what the woman says to him. But to her great relief he does not appear annoyed with her or so disappointed as she expected him to show himself. It does not seem as if he had found his martyrdom as wasted, quite, as she supposes it to be. Giving the woman money—more than the price of the smokes he has *not* had, Tartar arranges to let her know when next he needs her help and nodding to her, speeds down the stairs with spirits rising with the morning and with the prospect of a busy day ahead.

First he makes for his chambers in Staple Inn, there to snatch a little sleep and have a bath and shave and breakfast. After that, at ten o'clock, he will go round to Grewgious' chambers, as arranged, to confer with him and Crisparkle.

On second thoughts, Tartar changes his programme slightly. Bazzard, it seems, is spying on them and may report the conference to Jasper. So ten o'clock finds Tartar smoking his after breakfast pipe on the seat that circles the centre tree of the front court clump watching for the Minor Canon to come in under the entrance arch from Holborn. Before his pipe is finished Crisparkle comes briskly in. Tartar greets him and then diverts him from his plan of going at once to Grewgious' chambers and carries him up instead to his own. He does not detain him long there. Just long enough to explain about Bazzard and to arrange for the Minor Canon to go alone to the conference with Mr. Grewgious and to invite the latter, in Bazzard's hearing, to meet " an old schoolfellow of his at an early dinner at

Furnivals." There the real plan of action can be formulated between them without fear of spying.

It is not necessary for us to follow in detail the intervening period. At Furnivals the three meet as arranged, and a rather long discussion between them produces a summary of the present position and the future plans somewhat to this effect :—All were now agreed that Edwin was dead, and that Jasper was his murderer. Clearly the motive was jealousy and love of Rosa. Mr. Grewgious disclosed the evidence he had on this point. There was Jasper's strange " God save them both." There was his white-lipped anxiety to learn whether Grewgious had been sent for to hear that the engagement was broken off. There was his reception of the news of the utter needlessness of the murder for its object after he had committed it. Last and most conclusive of all there was his mad confession when making love to Rosa. Mr. Crisparkle, too, recalled Jasper's delirious cry " What is the matter ? " " Who did it ? " when he disturbed him sleeping. Tartar added what he had been able to gather from the fragments overheard by the opium woman threatening danger to " Ned," and plainly disclosing Jasper's wild love for the threatened young man's sweetheart. Granted the murder, it must have been accomplished between the time of Neville's good-night to Edwin, and the time next morning when Jasper came shouting for his nephew. Mr. Crisparkle suggested that Jasper had somehow induced Edwin to go with him down to the river and there had drowned him.

But Tartar had another theory. He had lately

improved his acquaintance with Durdles the Stone-mason. Aided by a large bottle of spirits, he had managed to extract from him in the course of several conversations a disjointed account of his journeyings with Jasper including in particular the unaccountable expedition on the Monday before the crime. Durdles' description was confused and blurred and puzzling to a degree, but these salient facts stood out from it. (1) That even before the murder—on this Monday—Neville was threatened by Jasper. Tartar's resumé of what took place behind the fragment of wall of Minor Canon Corner, was supplemented by Mr. Crisparkle's recollection of what took place in front of it. Neither the Minor Canon nor Neville had any suspicion of being watched that night. (2) That Jasper showed a quite inexplicable interest in the keys that Durdles carried ; especially it would seem in the key tied up in Durdles' bundle which opened Mrs. Sapsea's tomb.

(3) That Jasper had deliberately got Durdles drunk and had then left him locked up in the crypt while he himself was somewhere outside the Cathedral. This fact was not realised by Durdles himself, but Tartar was sure of it. His confidence was based on a singular fact derived from Deputy—the Imp. Deputy had seen Jasper entering the crypt that Monday night, alone, less than an hour before the time he earned the enmity of the Imp by " a-histing him off his legs," and nearly choking him. Durdles too remembered being shaken in his sleep and " dropping " the crypt key. Durdles also noticed that his bundle in which he carried the Sapsea key was not tied as he himself always tied it.

H

Mr. Crisparkle, at this point, suggested an immediate search of the Sapsea tomb in the expectation of finding Edwin's body in it. But Tartar went on to explain that he had taken the liberty of borrowing Durdles' key without his knowledge and had searched the tomb himself already, but to his own intense surprise had found nothing at all unusual within it—" except," he said " a very small trace of lime left lying there." Mr. Grewgious here interposed that he was afraid that they were going to find themselves up against a most serious legal difficulty. Satisfied as they were—satisfied as any jury might be—that the boy was murdered and murdered by Jasper, yet no judge would allow a jury to convict unless some part at least of the body could be found, to prove the death. It looked to him as if in this case the body had been successfully and entirely destroyed or got rid of.

Here again Mr. Tartar had clues and suggestions which he thought might help them. Mr. Grewgious was of course aware from Mr. Crisparkle of the painful disclosure that Jasper had made that morning from which it appeared that Mr. Grewgious' confidential clerk Bazzard had betrayed his employer. There could be no doubt that Bazzard was secretly communicating with Jasper about the mystery. Mr. Grewgious had not, by chance, commissioned Bazzard to do this for the sake of securing evidence had he? No! emphatically Mr. Grewgious had not done that. Could Mr. Grewgious throw light at all on Jasper's reference to Bazzard? The words were—" the clue is found. The link. The ring. I will go get it.

Now! to-night! It **did** not come back. **Bazzard** is certain."

"Yes." Mr. Grewgious thought he knew exactly what was meant. A ring of diamonds and rubies in a gold setting which had belonged to Miss Rosa's mother **was** entrusted to him by Miss Rosa's father to give to Mr. Edwin, her betrothed, to be their engagement ring if they married. This ring Mr. Grewgious had handed to Edwin for that purpose in the presence of Bazzard. When handing the ring to him Mr. Grewgious had thought it right to charge Edwin very solemnly that if anything were at all amiss between him and Miss Rosa instead of giving the ring to her, he should bring it back to Mr. Grewgious. Bazzard, Mr. Grewgious believed, was sleeping while this solemn injunction to bring the ring back was laid upon Edwin, but the clerk had wakened immediately afterwards and at Mr. Grewgions' request had formally witnessed the transaction. Mr. Grewgious had since ascertained that the ring had not been given to Miss Rosa or even mentioned to her; nor had it been returned to Mr. Grewgious.

Mr. Tartar was clear, after what Mr. Grewgious had told them, that Bazzard had revealed to Jasper about the ring, its gift to Edwin and its non-return.

Mr. Crisparkle now asked how it was that the ring was not with the watch and pin which he had found at Cloisterham Weir, and what interpretation could be put upon the rest of Jasper's ravings? With regard to the Weir, Tartar put a few questions to Mr. Crisparkle which at once brought out that he frequently visited the Weir for bathing. This made it **not** unreasonable to

suppose that the jewellery had been left there by Jasper
for the express purpose of its being found by the Minor
Canon. The ring, on the other hand was, it seemed,
unknown to Jasper and might not have been discovered
by him when he took the watch and pin from the body.
Had Mr. Grewgious communicated the trust on which
he held the ring to Jasper ? No. It was mentioned
in the will of Mr. Bud, but so far as Mr.. Grewgious was
aware, Jasper had never seen this will. An attested
copy of it had been sent to Rosa, and another to Edwin,
but none to Jasper. " Then," said Mr. Tartar " it
seems that Jasper knew of the rest of the jewellery and
removed it, but did not know of this ring till yesterday.
" It must still lie there." What can this mean except
that the ring must still lie where the body was left ?
If that be so Jasper intends to visit the spot at once—
to-night it may be—to secure the ring. He must be
followed. I will follow him.

Mr. Tartar then appealed to the lawyer to know
whether, supposing Jasper caught in the act of bearing
away a ring which Mr. Grewgious could identify as the
ring he had given to the lad who had so mysteriously
disappeared and bearing it away at night from a place
which was found to contain some trace of human remains
these facts coupled with circumstantial evidence of guilt,
of motive and of opportunity might not be sufficient to
overcome the legal difficulty arising from the absence of
the body of the vanished lad ? Would not the case be
allowed to go to a jury if these facts could be proved ?
" Yes," Mr. Grewgious thought in those circumstances
that the Judge might not feel bound to direct acquittal.

He was not certain but he thought so. In the circumstances of this case the ring would form very strong evidence of identity.

Mr. Crisparkle next called attention to those other words which Jasper used. Who was "the lawful prey?" Mr. Grewgious gravely feared it must mean Neville. It looked to him as if Jasper hoped to use the ring to assist him in bringing a charge of murder against Neville. Mr. Tartar had indeed rendered them a service by adventuring himself into this fearful den and learning what he had told them.

Tartar believes that the whole of Jasper's raving is now understood except the last ejaculation "Father and Son." There seems to be no context to throw light on that. Besides he cannot be quite positive that he heard the words aright. His movement of surprise on hearing Bazzard named had interrupted Jasper. A pity that. Otherwise he might have heard something really conclusive. However, they must act on the materials they had at present and hope that their inferences are the right ones. It would assist Mr. Tartar to make his own plans if he might be told those of the others for to-night and to-morrow? By all means. The Minor Canon travels down to Rochester this afternoon with Miss Landless and Miss Twinkleton who has been chaperoning Miss Rosa in London as Mr. Tartar no doubt knows. And Mr. Landless and Miss Bud? asks Tartar. Neville will remain in his chambers here and Miss Bud is to spend the next few days at Furnivals while arrangements are being concluded for her future residence by Mr. Grewgious. "I see," says

Mr. Tartar. " Well, I was proposing to sail my yacht
to Gravesend this afternoon, as the wind serves, and then
to take a coach and chaise to Rochester. Would it
not be well if Mr. Landless came with me ? The sea
air will do him no harm, and with his local knowledge
and having been the last person to see young Drood
alive he may be able to give me great assistance in
Rochester. He need not fear recognition for it will
be quite dark by the time we arrive, and he, Lobley and
I will go straight to my rooms where he will meet no
one else." Mr. Crisparkle undertakes to make this
suggestion to Neville, but doubts if he will feel inclined
to fall in with it as he is very loth to be seen in Rochester
after what has happened. Mr. Grewgious remarks that
he thinks it Landlesses' duty to go if there is any
possibility of his being of assistance to Mr. Tartar by
going.

Before the luncheon party breaks up it is arranged
that Mr. Crisparkle shall at once go openly to visit
Neville while Mr. Tartar, after a short interval, shall
return to his own chambers and then join Mr. Crisparkle
and the Landlesses by climbing out of his own window
and in at theirs. The only task of Mr. Grewgious for
the present will be to arrange for Rosa's future and to
keep a watch on Bazzard.

The scheme is carried out. The whole story is
laid before Helena and Neville and the plans made
clear to them. Neville surprises the Minor Canon by
seeming almost glad to leave Staple Inn for a while in
spite of Rosa being at Furnivals. He seems depressed
and dispirited but as Tartar's story proceeds, grows

furious against Jasper and more than once gives way to that motion of clenching his right hand which Mr. Crisparkle dislikes so much. As a concession to Neville's not unnatural dread of being seen and recognised in Rochester, Tartar undertakes to supply a disguise for him and it is arranged that Helena shall take down with her an outfit of her brother's usual clothing. Rosa, it is decided need not be told the plans at present. They hope to have something more definite to tell her by to-morrow.

Having now completed our summary of the dawn's disclosures, and the day's discussions, we will adjourn the scene from Staple Inn to Rochester, where all the party now in Neville's room are to meet again before the next day dawns.

EPISODE X.
HELENA'S PART.

EPISODE X.

HELENA'S PART.

A N unusually handsome lithe young fellow and an unusually handsome lithe girl; much alike; both very dark and very rich in colour; she of almost the gypsy type; something untamed about them both; a certain air upon them of hunter and huntress; yet withal a certain air of being the objects of the chase rather than the followers. Slender, supple, quick of eye and limb; half shy, half defiant; fierce of look, an indefinable kind of pause coming and going on their whole expression, both of face and form, which might be equally likened to the pause before a crouch or a bound. The rough mental notes made in the first five minutes of his acquaintance with them by Mr. Crisparkle would have read thus verbatim. Neville's own short history of himself and his sister was as follows : " We come (my sister and I), from Ceylon. We are twin children. Our mother died there when we were little. We lived with a stepfather and have had a wretched existence. He was a miserly wretch who grudged us food to eat and clothes to wear and a cruel brute who beat my sister more than once or twice. My sister would have let him tear her to pieces before she would have let him believe that he could make her shed a tear. Nothing in our misery ever subdued her, though it often cowed me. When we ran away from it (we ran

away four times in six years to be soon brought back
and cruelly punished), the flight was always of her
planning and leading.   Each time she dressed as a boy
and showed the bearing of a man.   I remember when
I lost the pocket-knife with which she was to have
cut her hair short how desperately she tried to tear it
out or bite it off."   A girl of remarkable character this
Helena.   True twin to her brother but without his
imperfections and weaknesses of character.   Rapid of
thought and action it is she, first, who comes to Rosa's
rescue at the piano.   Quick of eye she alone first fathomed
Jasper's secret love for Rosa and Rosa's fear and detes-
tation of him.   Bold of speech she endorses Edwin's
conventional remark that Rosa's music master has made
her afraid of him and her endorsement gives it meaning.
Bolder still she says outright that she herself would not
fear Jasper under any circumstances.   How little then
she thought under what circumstances of terror she was
to prove her courageous fearlessness of him !   But there
was a slumbering gleam of fire in the intense dark eyes
that night when in the privacy of their own room she
took the frightened Rosa under her strong protection.
Let whomsoever it might concern look well to it !

Jasper has cause to be apprehensive of fierce Helena,
not alone as protectress of Rosa, but also as protectress
and avenger of her brother.   She notices what others
do not see " Oh, Mr. Crisparkle," she asks " would you
have Neville throw himself at young Drood's feet or at
Mr. Jasper's, who maligns him every day ? "   After the
disappearance, Jasper shews that he is, in truth, a trifle
apprehensive of Helena by his question to Grewgious

"Have you seen "—not Neville, but—" his sister ? "
to learn in answer that she is defiant of all suspicion and
has unbounded faith in her brother. Her sustained
confidence in Neville and the truth is such that after
Neville himself is cowed and broken by the better sort
of people averting their eyes and silently giving him
too much room to pass when he meets them in the streets
of Rochester, Helena passes along those self same
streets boldly and as high in the general respect as any
one who treads them. She proves herself a truly brave
woman whom nothing can subdue. Nothing ! To
meet a man whom you know to be a murderer and to
meet him unarmed and alone requires great courage.
To meet him at night more courage. But to meet him
alone, unarmed, at dead of night, in the tomb of his
murdered victim and to be yourself dressed like the
victim is to meet him under circumstances bound
(one would think), to be terrifying to anyone—let alone
an unprotected girl. Under these circumstances of
terror Helena meets Jasper and is undaunted. She
stands alone in the tomb awaiting him. Her rôle is
Edwin Drood. Wearing her brother's clothes she
hopes in the darkness of the tomb to seem to Jasper a
second Edwin.

What can have brought this pair of enemies at this
strange hour in this strange guise to this strange place ?
What is Jasper seeking here ? Why does Helena await
him thus ?

"Father and Son." Those words had baffled
Tartar and the rest. Turning them over and over in
her mind as she travelled down to Rochester, Helena

had hit upon their meaning. Edwin was the son. Had Edwin's parents long been dead before his disappearance, she asks the Minor Canon? Mr. Crisparkle answered that he had never known Edwin's mother. His father died some years before him and was buried at Rochester. " Father and son together ! " Helena sees it in a flash ! Her first inclination is to tell the Minor Canon her suspicions and to have the grave of the elder Drood examined. But then it occurs to her that even if they do discover the body of Edwin in that tomb and the ring as well, still they will have no proof that Jasper was the murderer. The wretch may even maintain his threat to Neville. Should Jasper be caught there visiting the spot might he not (in a Court of Law) evade the inference that would hang him? Suppose he boldly asserted that he came there seeking evidence—as a detective? It is well known that he pretends to be tracking down the murderer. Nothing but a full confession, Helena thinks, will really hang him or save her brother. Led by her reasoning to this difficult conclusion, Helena is nonplussed at first. At last she has it ! Supernatural dread may extort from the villain's conscience a confession. In her troubled childhood, more than once, Helena has dressed herself in her brother's clothing. She will do so again and in the darkness of the tomb, and the guiltiness of Jasper's conscience, she will seem to him like the murdered Edwin. The plan once formed, nothing will turn Helena from it. She knows full well, however, that on no account would the Minor Canon allow it, therefore, saying nothing to him of her resolve, she acts alone and secretly.

EPISODE XI.

FLIGHT AND PURSUIT.

EPISODE XI.

FLIGHT AND PURSUIT.

MIDNIGHT is echoing under Jasper's vaulted gateway. The postern door opens. Cautiously Jasper himself comes out. He glances round him suspiciously, but all is silent in the High Street and the Cathedral Precincts are empty. Hastening to the churchyard with quick but stealthy tread, he unlocks the Drood sarcophagus, and, once within it, shuts the door and lights his lantern. Stepping through an unlocked inner door holding the lantern high above his head, its feeble rays fall sharply on the slim and youthful figure of a man. This can't be real! Jasper must be dreaming. Edwin come to life! Is it a ghost that stands before him motionless and silent its left hand in the breast of the long top coat as if seeking some object in the pocket? A ghost—pshaw! A mental fancy. Suddenly the hand shoots out holding in its palm a ring! The action betrays the figure and Jasper now knows it for no fancy and no ghost. Glaring along the feeble candle rays he thinks he knows the face and figure—yes and the clothing! Neville Landless! Jasper your chance is come. Your enemy is delivered into the grip of your strong fingers. The lamp is shattered in the first fierce onset, and the struggle goes on in darkness and in silence save for the gasps for breath and cracking joints and shuffling feet. The

outcome of it all is obvious from the start. With the
last choking breath a feeble cry escapes the victim.
A female cry, the voice of a woman! Relaxing, too
late, his iron grip Jasper learns the truth. His second
victim is a woman. Neville lives still to be the avenger
of his murdered sister. The limp body of the murdered
girl collapses to the floor while Jasper dazed and reeling
gropes in the darkness for the outer door and stumbles
forth from the tomb into the night air—straight into the
arms of Neville Landless.

This new situation requires a word of explanation.
When Jasper issued from his gatehouse door at midnight, and looked around suspiciously for watchers,
he little thought how near they were to him. No light
shone through the ground floor window of Mr. Datchery's lodging, but there he sat behind the darkened
window still guarding the archway door like a cat guards
mousehole. With him are Landless and Lobley, silently
awaiting his signal. The signal is given as soon as Jasper
has gone on towards the Cathedral, and the three con-
spirators come out and follow him. Triumphant they
mark him select and enter the Drood sarcophagus and
close the door. Unknown to one another, the Precincts
were alive that night with many hiding figures. We
have seen Helena inside the tomb awaiting Jasper.
Behind the North door of the crypt Crisparkle and
Durdles lie in hiding. The Imp too, we may be sure,
is lurking somewhere near. But to return to the three con-
spirators awaiting Jasper's exit from the tomb, all unsus-
pecting of the tragic struggle going on within it. They
hope to arrest him with the ring upon him issuing from

the unsuspected hiding place of Edwin's body. They anticipate a stealthy hurried exit. Instead of which Jasper bursts upon them heedless of anything, and in a state approaching frenzy. As Neville, who is nearest, seizes him, he does not struggle, but shouts aloud " her brother," in a voice of terror. " She is dead, dead, dead. In there," . . . and points. Without a syllable in answer, Neville loosing Jasper hurries within the open tomb. Datchery follows him and Lobley. Jasper makes no move, attempts no escape but does not enter. They carry Helena forth and lay her body down outside. Then with a dire and bitter cry for vengence Neville springs at Jasper who turns and flees, his undirected steps carrying him among the graves towards the Cathedral. Brought forth by the cry, Durdles and Crisparkle issue from the crypt and join in the pursuit of Jasper. Doubling back Jasper darts in at the crypt door left open and up the Great Tower's winding stair-case. Up and up the twisting stairs [1] two steps at a time close after Jasper comes Neville ; then Datchery, Lobley, Crisparkle [2] and heavy Durdles last. Anon they turn into narrower and steeper staircases and the night air begins to blow upon them and frightened rooks fly out and wheel around. When they gain the open,

[1] *Up the Twisting Stairs.* See the note upon the cover. (*Appendix V*).

[2] *Datchery, Lobley, Crisparkle.* This is my reading of the cover. The top figure has Datchery's wig and Tartar's agility ; the bottom one has clothes of a clerical cut ; the centre one has a lot of hair and ill-suits any of the better-known characters ; there is nothing inconsistent, however, with his being " the dead image of the sun in old wood-cuts, his hair and whiskers answering for rays all round him," or " a jolly favoured man with tawny hair and whiskers."

top Neville the hunter is hard on Jasper. As stag at bay turns on the hounds, Jasper turns on Neville. The rôles are now reversed, and the pursued hunts his pursuer round the narrow passage at the Tower top; but not for long.

Exhausted, Neville stumbles, a push from Jasper and—look down, look down, you see what lies at the bottom there! The appalling death yell rings in the ears of the fellow huntsmen as they too reach the fresh night air. Was it Jasper? Fear tells their hearts it was not. Left alone upon the tower top, the murderer is nerved by desperation to a feat else never attempted. No less than to seek escape by climbing down the tower side to gain the leads over the cathedral roofing. Tartar gains the open top only to find it empty. Lobley next joins him there, then Crisparkle. The rim of moon that is yet to come, has not risen. They can make out nothing. All three listen. Yes! The scrambling sounds, the labouring breath, the falling pieces, must mean that. Someone is climbing in the darkness down the tower face. Appalled they look towards one another. The cry was Neville's. This scrambling maniac is a triple murderer. Crisparkle is prostrated by the tragedies. Tartar, accustomed to emergencies takes command. Lobley he despatches for two bell-ropes from the belfry. Durdles he sends back to the ground to find the body and collect assistance; some to watch the tower base, others to join them at the top. Lobley returning with the ropes, the Minor Canon regains his self command and assists the two to fasten the ropes to a stanchion which Tartar has found there. Tartar then prepares to make the descent. He and Lobley test the ropes and then, whilst Crisparkle assists above, the pair slide down [3] them. Crisparkle himself follows the sailors when other help has reached him on the tower top. Not to prolong the agony, Jasper between them all is cornered and encircled and brought to solid ground a handcuffed prisoner. Helena, meanwhile, they have carried to Minor Canon Corner, and to the joyful surprise of all she is found to be still living. The China Shepherdess setting aside the keen anxiety for " her Sept," she feels, soothingly tends Helena with heated blankets and with cordials from the wondrous closet.[4] Slowly her persistent tending is rewarded with signs of returning life and consciousness in the patient. Helena returns to life.

Poor Neville's crushed remains are carried to the still open tomb—as to a mortuary—there to await the morning. No trace of Edwin has been found within.

So ends the tragic night with the mystery still unsolved. For where is Edwin ?

---

[3] *Slide Down*. This portion about the Tower top is not inserted for the mere sake of melodrama. There is more than one hint of some such conclusion. " Landless who was himself, I think, to have perished in assisting Tartar to unmask and seize the murderer." Forster, Life, etc. Compare also the climbing scenes at Neville's chambers and the scattered references to the agility of the Minor Canon.

[4] *The Wonderous Closet*. This was a personal recollection of Charles Dickens himself. The closet entry in the manuscript reads :—" The closet, I remember, there as a child, " *not* " remember there is a child."

THE MANUSCRIPT ENDS.

THE MANUSCRIPT ENDS.

WHAT more have I to tell ?   That I have been tried for my crimes, found guilty and sentenced.   That I have not the courage to anticipate my doom or to bear up manfully against it.   That I have no compassion, no consolation, no hope, no friend.   That I am alone in this stone dungeon with my evil spirit, and that I die to-morrow. To-morrow ? The dawn has broken. I die to-day.

Postscript in Another Hand.

THIS book of death was found in the condemned cell of Maidstone Gaol, in 1844, addressed simply "To Rosa." Remaining unclaimed, it found its way at last into the Gaol Museum of ghastly relics.   Had the writer not chanced upon it there, the story might have remained unread until the Day on which all things secret shall be revealed.   On a small stone slab in the prison cemetery is cut " JOHN JASPER, 1843."

It happens that the writer knew some of the persons mentioned in the murderer's tale (all long since dead), and so can add a fact or two to round their history off.

The Mystery was solved by means of Durdles' curious gift (or skill as he preferred to call it) of sounding sepulchres. His sounding of the elder Drood's sarcophagus led to the discovery of lime within the cavity of which he had spoken to Jasper. When this was opened up, a ring—a rose of diamonds and rubies delicately set in gold—flashed brightly back the rays of lantern light. The lasting beauty of those stones was almost cruel. The lime was analysed, and mixed with it was found sufficient trace of mortal remains of human origin to permit the jury at the trial to " find " a body. Nay, more—to find the body of Edwin Drood, foully murdered by the prisoner in the dock, John Jasper.

Among the mighty store of wonderful chains that are for ever forging day and night in the vast ironworks of time and circumstance, there was one chain forged in the moment of that small conclusion (which Edwin reached to let the jewels lie unspoken of in his breast), which was riveted to the foundations of heaven and earth, and gifted with invincible force to hold and drag. That chain, riveted by the ring to the earth's foundations, and linked by eternal justice to the heavens, held Jasper fast and dragged him to the gallows. But for that small conclusion Jasper might not have been convicted even of Neville's murder, which might have been an accident, for no one saw him given the fatal push.

Helena did not die. Thanks (as the China Shep-herdess to her dying day declared), to the magic of the marvellous closet and its cordials she soon, and quite recovered. Indeed she lived to call the Minor Canon (then the Dean) " her " Sept and the China Shepherdess " Mamma."

Rosa never received a third proposal. Man proposes but . . . Rosa was disposed of to Lieutenant Tartar on the day when, crossing the wide street of Holborn, on the sailor's arm, and happening to raise her eyes to his far-seeing blue ones looking, she thought, as if they had been used to watch danger afar off, and to watch it without flinching drawing nearer and nearer, her dark eyes saw with sudden embarrassment, that he too seemed to be thinking something about *them*. This a little confused Rosebud, and may account for her never afterwards quite knowing how, formally, he became the Lord High Admiral, and she became His Lady, the First Fairy of the Sea. The ring he put upon her finger was a plain gold circle. The tragic ring of diamonds and rubies returned undimmed to Mr. Grewgious' keeping. Who has it now, I wonder?

APPENDICES.

APPENDIX I.

EXTRINSIC EVIDENCE.

We know from Charles Dickens himself, from his son, and from his biographer, that Jasper did murder Edwin Drood. We know from his illustrator how he murdered him.

(1) *Dickens' Manuscript Notes.* In his own handwriting, and for his own eye alone, Dickens wrote (a) " Murder very far off," and (b) " Lay the ground for the manner of the murder to come out at last."

(2) " Mr. Charles Dickens informed me . . . that Edwin Drood was dead. His (Mr. Dickens') father told him so himself." W. R. Hughes : *A Week's Tramp in Dickens Land.*

(3) " The story . . was to be that of the murder of a nephew by his uncle ; discovery by the murderer of the utter needlessness of the murder for its object was to follow hard upon commission of the deed." Forster : *Life of Charles Dickens.*

(4) We know from Sir Luke Fildes exactly how Jasper murdered Edwin. " I must have the double necktie ! It is necessary, for Jasper strangles Edwin Drood with it." This was the answer Dickens gave when his attention was called to the change he had made in Jasper's dress from a little black tie once round the neck to a large black scarf of strong close woven silk, slung loosely round it. (See the artist's very important and interesting letter to *The Times* on this subject in October, 1905).

APPENDIX II.

THE DATE OF THE STORY.

The murder took place precisely at midnight, 24-25 December, 1842. The reader is no doubt astonished at this confident assertion. So was the author to discover the evidence on which he bases it.

Speaking approximately, the book itself proves the disappearance to have been on a Christmas Eve which was a Saturday. If any precise year was intended, therefore, it must have been one in which Christmas Day fell upon a Sunday. We can narrow the choice of year still further. In those days there was no railway to Cloisterham, and Mr. Sapsea said there never would be. Some remote fragment of main line to somewhere else, there was. Now Christmas fell upon a Sunday in 1836, in 1842 and in 1853. In 1836 no remote fragment of line to

anywhere else approached near Rochester...By 1853 the line to Strood
was built. The line to Strood cannot have been the "fragment"
referred to. It was not remote. It was not a fragment of main line
to anywhere else. It could not have so unsettled Rochester traffic that
the traffic deserting the high road, came sneaking in from an unprecedented part of the country by a back stable way. If any precise year
was intended therefore, it can only have been 1842. But was it?

In the year of the book (if it had a year), no neighbouring architecture of lofty proportions had arisen to overshadow Staple Inn.
The Westering sun bestowed bright glances on it and the South-west
wind blew into it unimpeded. By 1853, this was no longer so. The
lofty building which is now the Patent Office standing in what was
once the garden of the Inn was planned in 1843, and built soon after.
Later the Birkbeck Buildings shut out the Western sun.

Six months or so after the murder, Mr. Crisparkle and Neville dined
together in London and then parted at the yet unfinished and un-
developed railway station; Mr. Crisparkle to get home to Rochester.
The British Almanac for the previous year, 1842, contains this entry:
" The great station at London Bridge, for the joint use of the Brighton,
South Eastern and Croydon companies, and the works connected with
it, are in rapid progress, but any description of them must be deferred
until their completion."

Finally. By 1842, a fragment of the Main Line to Maidstone had
been completed and was in use as far as a station then called " Maidstone Road," which will be seen from the map to be the point on that
line nearest to Rochester. " I lost ye last, where that omnibus you got
into nigh your journey's end plied betwixt the station and the place,"
the opium woman apostrophises Jasper. Maidstone Road was " the
station," and Rochester " the place." The omnibus containing
Jasper came sneaking in to Rochester from this unprecedented part
of the country (the new railway station) by a back stable way which
was then Crow or Crau Lane, but is now the Maidstone Road.

The year 1842, then, is a probable year; it is the only possible
year; and it is a year which accords in a quite remarkable fashion
with a number of hints contained in the book. In fact the assertion
is justified that 1842 was the year intended by Dickens.

APPENDIX III.

THE DATCHERY ASSUMPTION.

Datchery, like Mr. Nadgett the investigator in " Martin Chuzzlewit," is " a man of mystery." Not that there is any doubt about his
occupation. The idle man is busy watching Jasper. The buffer of
an easy temper is playing the detective. His reason for this busy

idleness is what requires an explanation—that, and who he is himself. He might be Bazzard, but in character he is that gloomy self-centred clerk's antithesis. He might be Edwin were not Edwin dead. He might be Helena, were she not a woman. He may be quite a stranger to the story. But the author is convinced that Datchery is Tartar.

If Datchery is not Tartar, we have perforce, another mystery with which to battle. Why did Tartar—who was in love with Rosa, and with whom Rosa was in love, and who was to marry Rosa, and whose chambers were within ten minutes' walk of Rosa's lodgings, and who was daily and hourly anticipated there by Rosa—never call on Rosa at the Billickin's ?

If Tartar is not Datchery, again, why is there nothing inconsistent in the personal descriptions of the two men ? Why in drawing one of them is it possible to describe the pair ? Why are their tastes odd and identical ? Why do these two characters employ closely similar phrases of polite apology ten times and all the other characters that Dickens drew not even once ? In a word why are their personalities so similar that a critic who (for other reasons) believed their identification to be *impossible* yet could write " Datchery's speech and bearing have a distinct individuality resembling that of no other person in the story except Tartar ? "

The Tartar theory has had one, and only one, serious objection brought against it. That objection is the sequence of the chapters.

CHAPTER XVII.   Tartar introduces himself to Landless and to us.

CHAPTER XVIII.   Datchery appears at Cloisterham.

CHAPTER XIX.   Jasper proposes to Rosa who faints in going upstairs.

CHAPTER XX.   Rosa flees to Staple Inn and confides in Mr. Grewgious.

CHAPTER XXI.   Rosa and Tartar meet for the first time and fall in love.

The explanation of the difficulty seems to be that Dickens intentionally departed from strict chronology in the marshalling of his Chapters. He jumps from place to place and not from time to time. Authors often do.

Chronologically everything hinges on the opening words of the Chapter that introduces Datchery to Cloisterham.

"At about this time a stranger appeared in Cloisterham." At about what time ? When the words were written the Chapter followed Rosa's fainting fit. They were not altered when the Chapter (for some reason possibly connected with the monthly issues) was put earlier.

At about the time of Rosa's fainting, then, Datchery appeared in Rochester. Why not ? Rosa fainted on Monday, July 3rd. On Tuesday, she met Tartar. On Wednesday, he vanished from the story as London-Tartar, and her gritty stage began. On this same

Wednesday, he became the man of mystery at Rochester. Does not an event on Wednesday occur " at about the time " of one on Monday ?

For a somewhat more detailed presentation of " The Case for Tartar " the author refers the reader to the pages of *The Dickensian*. In them will be found articles in January 1906, by Mr. G. F. Gadd, and in October, 1919, by the present author.

APPENDIX IV.

DURDLES' YARD.

So far as the author's researches have extended, no one yet has identified the site of Durdles' house.

Durdles, it will be remembered, was a stonemason, chiefly in the gravestone, tomb, and monument way, who lived in a little antiquated hole of a house that was never finished, and was supposed to be built so far of stones stolen from the City wall. To this abode there was an approach ankle deep in stone chips, and resembling a petrified grove of tomb stones, urns, draperies and broken columns in all stages of sculpture. By the yard gate there lay, on the night of the unaccountable expedition, a mound of quick-lime, " Quick enough to eat your boots, with a little handy stirring, quick enough to eat your bones."

Now, according to Forster, " by means of a gold ring which had resisted the corrosive effects of the lime into which he had thrown the body, not only the person murdered was to be identified, but the locality of the crime, and the man who had committed it."

How, then, came the lime from Durdles' Yard into the place of sepulture ? In Procter's opinion, " either then, while Durdles slept " (in the crypt on the night of the unaccountable expedition) " or on the night of the murder, Jasper procured some of this quick-lime and put it in Mrs. Sapsea's tomb." This opinion the present author shares. By the majority, of recent students of the Mystery, however, this hypothesis has been scouted on the grounds thus forcefully stated by Professor Henry Jackson in his invaluable study " About Edwin Drood."

" I demur altogether to the hypothesis which Mr. Lang shares with Mr. Procter, that Jasper brought quick-lime in a wheel barrow from one end of Cloisterham to the other. Anyone who is acquainted with Rochester will perceive that the route through the Monk's Vineyard would have dangers as great as those of the route along the High Street though no doubt of a different kind."

The author recalls the tale of a logic lecturer at an Oxford College, who (by way of illustrating the many means of escape from a logical dilemma), notionally blocked the doors and windows of the Hall in which he was lecturing with armed murderers, and then lighted an inextinguishable fire within. Having convinced his audience that he had left himself no means of escape, he next touched a secret spring in the oak pannelling behind him and concluded his lecture by disappearing from the room.

It is even so with the dilemma with which Dickens has puzzled Professor Jackson and the rest. From the graveyard there are but two orthodox approaches to Durdles' hole-in-the-wall—the one *via* the Vines, the other through the High Street. Both routes are impossible for the secret carriage of quick-lime. But a third and hidden route offers every facility. For in truth Durdles' unfinished house which actually abuts on the Precincts, may be described in a sense as "over-looking the churchyard." Dickens so described it himself in his manuscript, but deleted the description before printing the number, perhaps from the fear that it gave too much away at that stage.

A glance at the plan of Rochester will shew the route taken by Jasper in carrying the lime to the grave which he intended for Edwin's occupation. The way is short, secret and easy, and leads through that "stillest part which the Cathedral overshadows," to which Jasper paid such unaccountable attention. Furthermore the lime explains why it was necessary for Jasper to arrange that Durdles should be away from home on that night, and also why he apprised the Dean (whose entrance drive he would have to use) of his intention to engage in these nocturnal prowlings. The whole device is redolent of the genius of simplicity.

The author places Durdles' Yard next to what is called "the Old Deanery." There used to be a builder's yard here, and in a painting in the Nun's house, it is indicated as such. The Old Deanery, which is well worth a visit for its own sake, is now a bookshop, and appears to be in the hands of a proprietor who takes a genuine interest in its architecture and associations. The entrance gate to the yard opens out on to the High Street, as that of Durdles' yard must have done. For when Jasper and he, on their way back *via* the Vines, came under the victorious fire of Deputy who was standing outside the Travellers' Twopenny, Jasper "turns the corner into safety and takes Jasper home." This corner was the junction of Crau Lane, with the High Street and after Durdles had stumbled up his stony yard to bed, Jasper returned to his Gatehouse "by another way," which was clearly the High Street also.

APPENDIX V.

THE COVER.

In a suggestive article in *The Dickensian* for January, Mr. Willoughby Matchett lays it down that "the true explanation of the cover lies less in the actual—that bee in the bonnet of all other solvers—than in the emblematical." Is Mr. Matchett right in this? Are the vignettes on the cover of purely emblematical significance or were they actual scenes in the story to be written ?   Mr. Matchett adds " Actual scenes were not the Dickens' custom."   But in this he is wrong. Amongst much emblematical matter woven into the decorative covers of Dickens' earlier books, several actual scenes are found.   The reader can verify this statement by consulting Mr. Matz Memorial Edition of Forster's " Life of Charles Dickens."   The covers are most conveniently collected there.

The truth is that the Drood cover is both emblematical and actual. The author's reading of it is as follows :—

Of the corner pieces, the top two are pure emblems ;   the bottom pair are characters in the story—a trifle idealized perhaps.   At the top, the spirit of happiness and roses is opposed by the sinister fury with a dagger.   At the bottom, while the Princess Puffer smokes her pipe in one corner, Jack-Chinaman-t'other-side-the-court enjoys his in the other.

On its sinister side, the cover is thorny and male ;   on its dexter side it is rosy and predominantly female.   Centrally, beneath the title, is Durdles dinner bundle surmounted by crossed key and spade.   The rest of the cover is occupied by actual scenes of which there are five.

(1) In the Nave of the Cathedral coming out from service with the choir, Jasper scrutinizes Rosa and Edwin walking arm-in-arm not over-lovingly.   Jasper's gaze is fixed on Rosa who looks away from him.

(2) A girl is studying a placard headed " LOST."   The author does not understand this scene, unless it is Rosa looking at one of Jasper's advertisements of Edwin's disappearance.

(3) A kneeling figure with moustache kisses the hand of a girl in a garden ; she, meanwhile, toys with a streamer from her hat in apparent embarrassment or boredom.   This is Neville proposing to Rosa in the garden of Staple Inn.

(4) A dark place in which a door has just been opened, admitting Jasper holding on high a lantern.   In the midst stands a statuesque figure dressed in a man's hat and a long coat and bearing some resemblance to the picture of Edwin higher on the cover.   Jasper seeking the ring finds Helena awaiting him there, in the tomb, dressed to resemble Edwin in Neville's garb.

(5) Three figures climb a winding staircase two steps at a time pointing upwards as they go.   They are Crisparkle, Lobley and Datchery (Tartar), pursuing Jasper up the staircase of the Tower.

Deacidified using the Bookkeeper process.
Neutralizing agent Magnesium Oxide
Treatment Date March 2009

PreservationTechnologies